T0319211

DUST AND RAIN
Chipo and Chibwe
save the Green Valley

Ruth Hartley

Gadsden Publishers

PO Box 32581, Lusaka

Cover painting and illustration on Part One:

Style Kunda

Other llustrations in text:

Ruth Hartley

ISBN 978-9982-24-127-4

DEDICATION

For Atara Leah, Ahava Ruth, Rivka Angela Thumelo,
Stephen Kupakwesu and children everywhere.

CONTENTS

PART ONE

THE FARM

CHAPTER ONE
THE WHIRLWIND

Something bad is going to happen.

My name is Chipo. Ma says I've a gift that allows me to feel things that other people can't. Maybe that's true. When I look up, I can see that the sky isn't blue. It's white-hot and so thick with dust that it makes it difficult to breathe. I know that something up there is watching us. Something is swirling up above us in circles that come closer and closer. I know it's not just the heat pressing on my head that makes me feel dizzy.

We all went out to help plough the fields this morning but the ground is so hard that Pa and Ma had to give up. They've gone back to the farmhouse leaving my brother, Chibwe, and me on our own with nothing to do. Chibwe is over twelve years old and I'm nearly eleven. Pa says Chibwe lives up to his name, which means a little rock, but Ma says Chibwe would do well to sometimes be like me.

"It's all very well being determined, Chibwe," Ma says. "It's a good idea to think first and use your common sense, like Chipo."

We made faces at each other when Ma said that but we don't often fight. More often we end up by doing something together like playing one-person-a-side football.

"Come on Chibwe!" I say after Ma and Pa have left. "I'm thirsty – let's find somewhere shady to sit by the river."

"It's too far to walk and I'm hungry," Chibwe says. "Let's look for bush fruit under the ilala palm trees instead."

That's one of our favourite places to play, so I agree.

"What happens if there is no rain and Pa and Ma can't grow any maize or vegetables this year?" I ask Chibwe. I know what will happen, of course. I've seen the worried looks on Pa and Ma's faces.

"We'll die of hunger – we'll starve," Chibwe says. Then he looks at me sideways and adds. "It's a joke, Chipo! We'll just eat less."

We start to run towards the Ilala palm trees and, as we do that, I feel as if the earth is lifting under my feet. Dead leaves and grass swish around our ankles and the air fills with blown sand.

"Watch out!" Ma calls out from the path back to the farmhouse. "There's a whirlwind coming our way!"

It is a really huge whirlwind. A towering tornado of dust, one of those strong circular winds that happen in the heat before the rainy season. They whip around tearing branches from trees and sometimes take the roofs off houses.

"Witches ride in these twisting dust storms," Grandmother Mutende once told us. "Point your little fingers at the whirlwind so the witch doesn't come close to you."

We laugh at her but we still do what she says.

"We've never seen a witch yet!" we tease.

"Wait and see!" she scolds, shaking her head at us. Then she adds "When witches fly through the air they never wear any clothes!"

That makes us laugh even more.

Chibwe and I easily reach the shelter of the palm trees but

this is such a powerful whirlwind that the Ilala palms are almost bent double and their leaves thrash close to our heads. We point our little fingers at the huge spiralling cloud of dirt, leaves and grass and then crouch down.

"Ow! That hurts!" says Chibwe as a stick slaps him. That's exactly the moment I see spinning around in the whirlwind, a shiny, shifting monster of a creature.

"Chibwe, look!" I scream. "It's a skeleton made of giant shiny worms!"

Chibwe stares. I hear his gasp. Human bones and wriggling sliding slithery creatures are coalescing into the shape of a person. It has two glowing yellow-green bulging eyes that seem to move around its head and blink rapidly without ever closing. Its gaze seems to fix on us, I hear a screech. My face is struck with gritty dust and I can't see anything any more.

My eyes are sore and stinging. Chibwe's are the same but rubbing them makes it worse. We have to wait until our eyes have watered enough to wash the grit out. I sit there with my hands over my face and try to think. My insides feel all shrivelled up and cold as if it's winter and not hot and dry.

"What did we see, Chibwe?" I ask. "Was that something or someone that fell out of an aeroplane?"

We do see aeroplanes here but they're so high they look very tiny.

"No," Chibwe says. "People don't fall out of planes but if they do they're still people and that wasn't a human person."

"Perhaps it was plastic rubbish that blew in from the city?" I say, thinking of all the strange shapes and shininess of plastic and how many different ways it can be used.

Chibwe and I made a football out of plastic and string we found around our school here. It doesn't bounce very well but it's good fun to kick about. When I was little, I put a plastic bag on my head as an experiment. I couldn't breathe. It was horrible and frightening. Ma told us that a goat in the village died from eating plastic bags.

"The city's too far away for anything to blow all the way here, besides whatever it was made a strange and angry noise when it saw us looking at it!" Chibwe answers.

The memory of the screech makes my stomach hurt even more.

"Let's go home." I say. "I want to see Ma and Pa."

"They'll be okay Chipo." Chibwe says. "Don't be silly."

He jumps up faster than me and we run home. There are still a few dry leaves floating around in the sky and there's dust everywhere. We slow down near the farmhouse though in case it looks as if we're worried. I stop to pick up the washing I hung out to dry early in the morning. It's blown off the boma – the fence around our yard.

"There's one chitenge cloth missing – that's lucky but also odd," I say. "It's Ma's favourite red piece of fabric that she wraps around her waist like a skirt when we have visitors."

Then Chibwe and I turn into the farmhouse yard.

CHAPTER TWO
KAMBILI

Ma and Pa have a guest.

I notice that Chibwe's eyes are still red with dust because they're so wide with surprise, then I realise my throat's dry and my mouth is hanging open. Wherever did this person come from? It doesn't seem possible that anyone could have arrived in the middle of that dust storm, especially not a young woman all alone. It's a very long, hot walk and there is no car outside. Here she stands, however, a very beautiful young woman, talking to Ma who has started to cook a meal even though it's hot and the middle of the day. There also is Pa, sitting in his chair under the tamarind tree. His face looks rather strange as if he has by accident bumped into an elephant in the bush. Perhaps he is half asleep, or dreaming. He looks as if someone has put a spell on him.

The young woman turns quickly around as we arrive. Her body seems to come apart then join together again as she moves. She becomes more solid as I watch. I duck behind Chibwe and pretend I'm too shy to look straight at her. Chibwe takes a step back and treads on my toes. I say "Ow!" very quietly and push against his back.

The young woman's eyes swivel around as if she is watching everywhere at the same time. A chameleon's eyes do the same very slowly but they are only looking for flies. The woman's eyes move fast and when they stop and fix on

Chibwe and me they burn right into us. I gasp, then hold my breath. The only thing she has wrapped around her to hide her naked body is Ma's favourite red chitenge cloth.

"Hello, children," the young woman says. "My name is Kambili. I expect you are good children and will listen to your parents."

I pinch the back of Chibwe's arm and whisper, "Who is she?"

"Hello Kambili," Chibwe says. "I didn't see you arrive."

He stops. Chibwe is always polite to other people.

Kambili laughs. "The dust got in your eyes, perhaps."

That makes me feel as if a spider was running down my back.

"Who ARE you?" I demand, sticking my head out from behind Chibwe.

Kambili turns towards me. At first, she moves like a leaf in a light breeze then her voice slams into me like a wind storm.

"I'm Kambili, child! Don't anger me! Ever!"

I'm blown back behind Chibwe but now I know who she is. I dig my fingers into Chibwe's back, stand on tiptoe and whisper in his ear.

"Kambili means 'Whirlwind' – she's a witch who travelled here in the dust storm!"

Chibwe turns and looks at me. He doesn't want to believe me. He looks at Pa. Pa's expression doesn't change. Ma is watching Kambili. Kambili is watching us. Chibwe frowns. He's wondering why Pa says nothing, so he tries a different question that he knows will interest Pa.

"Pa," Chibwe asks, "what are we going to do if we can't plough the field and plant our maize?"

Pa has a fly on his face that he doesn't brush away.

"Kambili will take care of everything," he answers, but his tongue seems to be swollen and his words are slow.

The spider isn't running down my back any more. but I do feel as if it bit me.

"Ma, what is happening?" I ask.

Kambili and Ma both turn to me. Kambili's eyes spin, then fix on me and burn but I can see that Ma is just as she is always. She speaks quietly to me and to Chibwe.

"Chipo, my daughter, thank you for bringing in the washing. Please go now and fetch us plates and cups and spoons so that we can all eat. Chibwe, brush the dust off the table and chairs."

"Do you think Kambili is going to stay here with us for long?" I whisper to Chibwe.

"It looks like it," he says. "Who is she? She's not a relative of ours, is she? She can't be a witch?" He sounds doubtful.

I shake my head. I don't know if I want to be told the truth.

"I'll ask Ma" I say, "when she's alone."

But that's the strangest thing. From that day onwards Chibwe and I never see our parents alone. Kambili is always with them or nearby. Whenever I start to ask Ma a question, Kambili's eyes are watching me. I think she can turn her head towards me even when her body is facing the other way. She is as quick as a striking snake. I am afraid of the power of her eyes. I think she has put Pa into a trance, because he just sits in the same place all day without doing any of the work that's needed on the farm. He doesn't look at Ma any more and he never stops staring at Kambili with his shocked eyes.

What's happening to my family? We have the very best parents in our farming district. Everyone who lives here respects them and comes to them for help and advice. They are very hard-working and very clever and they expect Chibwe and me to be the same. Ma is the best traditional healer and herbalist in the whole of our neighbourhood.

"Do you remember what Pa told us about education being important for success? He always said work hard at school and earn the respect of your friends. He always said show respect to your family and your elders." Chibwe says. "Now he isn't even asking us to go to school."

"Maybe we're too poor because of the drought," I say.

Ever since Kambili arrived the weather has got hotter and drier and dustier. Everything here at home seems upside-down and wrong since the day of the whirlwind.

"Pa hasn't mended anything that got broken in the wind," Chibwe says. "Let's go out pick up the rubbish that blew into the yard and sweep it clean."

We go outside and tidy up the yard but the next day we find the yard is dirty again and the same rubbish is back in exactly the same places.

"If only it would rain! If it rained Kambili would have to leave us and go away," I complain to myself. I knew that something dreadful was flying over us on the day of the whirlwind but that doesn't give me any power over the weather or Kambili.

I am starting to have a sick feeling in my stomach that maybe Kambili can change the weather. But if that's true, why would she want to make us suffer from such a terrible drought? It isn't as if it is our fault or as if there is anything we can do that would make it better.

"I hate Kambili. I really hate her!" I say to Chibwe. "What is happening to our family, Chibwe? What can we do about it?"

Chibwe is throwing stones at the scraggy-looking chickens trying to scratch up food in our yard. There's nothing much left for them to find.

"Leave them alone!" I say. "Not even the jackal will bother with those."

A couple of days ago a starving jackal came right into the yard and killed a cockerel. Kambili screeched so loudly at the skinny beast that it dropped it.

"Cook it!" Kambili instructed.

The cockerel was all bones and skin but we were so hungry we ate every single bit of it.

"Put out traps to catch field mice," Kambili ordered and Chibwe and I obeyed. We made little baskets baited with seeds and wove thorny twigs around them. Mice can get in to eat the seeds but they can't get out again. We'd never eaten mice before Kambili arrived and this time we only caught a few.

"What does she want them for?" I asked Chibwe.

"She wants the mice to put into the kachasu drink," Chibwe tells me. "I think it's got rubbish and poison and rats in it too!"

Kambili has been giving Pa beer every day and any time of day that he wants it. Ma used to make home-made maize beer for special feasts like weddings and funerals and harvest time but neither Pa or Ma ever drank much of it. Now Kambili is distilling kachasu by a special secret method for Pa. Kachasu is a very strong, alcoholic drink that smells horrible.

"What does she make it from?" I asked Chibwe a few days ago. "We don't have any maize left."

We both know the thatched grain store where we put our maize crop is empty except for a few husks.

Chibwe keeps trying to talk to Pa and tell him not to drink the kachasu but Pa just shakes his head and says things like "Later, Chibwe, later!" or "I'm busy now," when he isn't doing anything but sitting still. As that's got worse, so has Chibwe's bad temper.

We look at each other and I start to cry.

"You're just a stupid, useless girl!" Chibwe hisses.

We've been fighting with each other all the time since Kambili arrived.

I run to Ma. She grabs my arm and hides my face in her skirt. Then she says in a quiet ordinary voice, "We don't cry, Chipo. We don't cry, Chipo, because we don't want to upset Kambili, do we?"

I wipe my eyes and snivelly nose on Ma's skirt and peep out. Kambili's eyes are fixed on me. I smile at her.

"Hello, Kambili," I say.

She doesn't seem to be able to guess what I'm thinking, so she turns back to stirring the kachasu. I must remember that. I must warn Chibwe to hide his feelings, too.

But I'm too late to do that.

Chibwe is so angry that he has gone up to Pa and started shouting. Chibwe has tears in his eyes and his voice is all squeaky because he's upset.

"Pa!" Chibwe cries. "Pa – don't you love us anymore? Don't you care about Chipo and me anymore? Ma is your wife, not Kambili! Why are you letting that horrible Kambili tell you what to do?"

I think that a miracle is happening. Pa's eyes also fill with tears. He turns his head and I know that he is looking at Chibwe and me as if we really are his children and he loves us. Ma's eyes shine but only for an instant. In the very next moment she comes to Chibwe and gently leads him away from Pa. Somehow Kambili has transported herself right beside Pa and has her hand on his shoulder. The light leaves Pa's face but Kambili's eyes blink and glow.

"Ah, such sweet and tender children," she says. Her voice is a blunt saw that's harsh and squealing at the same time. "Such tasty, mice-like children, succulent little mice children, such a pleasing meal to feed a hungry Pa Mulenga and Ma Chiluba."

That's when I know, and Chibwe knows, and Ma knows that Kambili is planning to do something really dreadful to Chibwe and me. If Kambili can make this drought happen what other magical powers does she have? Can she put a spell on us? Can she control us as she controls Pa? Can she change us? Can Kambili turn us into mice and make Ma and Pa eat us?

CHAPTER THREE
CHIBWE AND CHIPO TALK

I look at Chibwe. He looks at me. Together we run as fast as we can from the house and from Kambili until we can hide underneath the ilala palm trees. My heart is thudding and even Chibwe is panting hard, but he is quicker than me and arrives first. This is where we first saw Kambili. I shudder and look up at the sky. There is no wind. It's just very hot and still.

"Are we safe here?" I ask.

"I shouldn't have got angry – should I?" Chibwe says.

He looks scared and sorry. I want to shout at him and tell him it's all his fault but he is the only other person I know who isn't under Kambili's control. I don't want to be completely alone and I've always relied on Chibwe. At least he does admit his mistake. I want to speak but a sob gets stuck in my throat. I'm trembling all over and I make a choking sound. Chibwe pats my shoulder.

"I'm angry too," I finally say. "It could have been me screaming at Pa or at Kambili instead of you."

"What will happen now?" Chibwe asks and then he adds, "What will happen to us? What will she do to us?"

"She said she is going to turn us into mice and then cook and eat us, didn't she? What can we do, Chibwe?"

"What is Ma doing? Why doesn't she help us?" Chibwe frowns.

For the first time we really sit down and talk about what is happening to our parents and to us.

"Kambili must have put a spell on Pa," Chibwe says.

"Yes," I agree. "What about Ma, though? Can't she send Kambili away? Why doesn't she stop her?"

Has our beloved Ma also fallen under Kambili's spell? Can we still trust her? I don't dare to ask Chibwe what he thinks, but instead Chibwe asks me that question himself.

"What about Ma – do you think Kambili controls her too?"

My stomach knots up and then unknots. I know the answer to that.

"I'm sure Ma is on our side and on Pa's side too."

"I don't think that Ma can make Kambili leave." Chibwe says. "I don't know if she can stop Kambili turning us into mice, either."

"Ma doesn't seem to be in a trance like Pa is. Why?"

Chibwe screws up his eyes.

"You know about that stuff Chipo, more than I do. Ma is a traditional healer and an herbalist. She has been teaching you how to use plants for medicines hasn't she?"

"So you think Ma is a special person and that stops Kambili having power over her like she has over Pa?"

"Ma's a good person." Chibwe says.

"Pa is too," I say.

We are both silent while we think about it.

"Should we run away from home?" I ask.

Chibwe pulls a face.

"Where would we go, Chipo? There's Ma's sister, Auntie Chimunya in the Big City but that's very far away and we can't walk there. We haven't got any money, either."

"Do you think Kambili would chase us? Would she let us run away? Perhaps she can still fly after us in her whirlwind?"

"I don't want to leave Pa and Ma," Chibwe says. "Will they both come with us?"

"Do you think Ma would come with us? Do we have to leave Pa behind with Kambili?"

"Ma would never do that!"

There are just too many questions for which we have no answers.

"We need to talk to her but we have to get her alone and that is going to be difficult."

"One of us will have to distract Kambili then and give the other a chance to speak to Ma," Chibwe says.

I nod. "It had better be me who distracts Kambili. She doesn't expect me to cause any trouble – not like you! Suppose Kambili can't read – perhaps we can write a message for Ma? Then we don't have to speak aloud and Kambili won't know what we say to Ma."

Together Chibwe and I make a plan. Now we have to carry it out.

CHAPTER FOUR
THE PLAN

"I'm going to read my schoolbooks," I say loudly, as I walk into the farmhouse without looking at Pa or Ma or Kambili. I find my school bag and carry it outside to where Chibwe is hiding. He grabs a pen, tears paper out of my notebook and begins to write. I sit where I can watch everyone while I read aloud from my story book. When Chibwe signals that he has finished the letter to Ma, I put my book down.

"Let's play five stones, Chibwe," I say. "I'm bored with reading."

We sit in the yard where we can be seen by Kambili and pretend that all we care about is competing to win the game. Chibwe beats me, of course, as we agreed.

"You cheated, Chibwe!" I shout and throw the stones down. "I'm going to sit with Pa."

Kambili's eyes swivel towards me and then fix. I sit down by Pa's feet. He doesn't move or notice me. I start to sing and clap my hands.

"What do good children do?

What do good children do?

We help our mothers in the house

We help our fathers in the field.

We sing and we dance."

I keep on singing and clapping. Ma looks once at me very quickly and turns her back so Kambili can't see her face.

Chibwe yawns and screws up his eyes.

"I'm going to lie down and sleep. It's too hot!" he says.

Chibwe starts to walk to his bed, passing close to Ma so that he can slip the folded letter into her hand as we planned, but Kambili stops looking at me, her eyes sharpen and spin towards him. In desperation I clap faster and sing louder and louder but Kambili carries on staring at Chibwe. We've had it, I think. We will be turned into mice. I'm so afraid that I start to forget the words and tune I'm singing. Then this amazing thing happens. Pa taps his knee as I sing and his body begins to rock.

"Aie! Good children help their fathers."

"Aie! Good children help their fathers," he chants.

It's not very good singing but it has a dramatic effect on Kambili. She turns right round and lifts up her hand in warning. I think she is going to hit Pa or make some frightening magic when suddenly Pa begins to speak. What he says is very strange, but it makes Kambili listen very carefully to every word he says. I see Chibwe behind her put his letter into Ma's hand and I see that she touches his head very gently in approval, but then, I too, have to listen to Pa.

"It's all our fault. The drought is all our fault," Pa says. "We've made the drought happen. We've burnt the grass. We've cut down the trees. We haven't looked after each other. We haven't looked after our land. We've drowned our valleys. We've given away our land for money to powerful, rich people who don't look after the earth and don't care if all the people die."

23

Kambili likes what Pa is saying. She nods at every sentence.

"Say it again," she shouts in her scraping sizzle of a voice. "And again."

I've stopped singing and clapping and that stops Pa speaking too. He seems to sink back again into his trance. Kambili isn't angry any more so I get up and go outside quietly. When I look back, I think that I see Ma smiling at me.

I must find Chibwe at once. Did he hear what Pa said? Did he see Kambili's reaction? What is happening? I don't understand anything.

CHAPTER FIVE
MA

"Chibwe!" I call. "Chibwe, did you hear what Pa said? Did you see what Kambili did? What do you think Ma will do when she reads our letter?"

Chibwe is really pleased with himself when I catch up with him.

"Did you see how clever I was?" he says. "I slipped the letter to Ma without Kambili seeing me do it."

"You did a good job of distracting Kambili, Chipo," he adds, as an afterthought.

"No, Chibwe! It wasn't me distracting Kambili! She nearly caught you anyway!"

Chibwe and I go back to sit under the ilala palm trees and I tell him all about Kambili's behaviour and what Pa said. Chibwe listens, frowning.

"Pa said that! Pa is a good farmer. Why did he say it was his fault? How strange that Kambili listened to him – do you think he means that Kambili is here because somehow we made her come?"

I try shaking the confusion out of my head.

"I only know that Kambili was pleased with what Pa said, but I can't understand why."

We are silent for a while.

"What about Ma, Chibwe?" I ask. "What do you think she will do?"

Then I change my question.

"What can Ma do?"

That makes us silent again.

My stomach starts to feel all jumpy. I sigh. It's bad enough having that hungry ache in it all the time but feeling nervous makes the pain worse. I know Chibwe feels the same, so I don't say anything. Neither does he.

We get up and walk back home slowly. There's nowhere else to go, after all. As we get closer to our yard, Chibwe takes my hand. It feels comforting. At that moment I see something that makes my heart skip with hope. I tug at Chibwe's hand.

"Sh!" I whisper, looking around in case Kambili sees us. "Be very quiet – but look Chibwe – what's that?"

On the side of the path, where it can't be seen from the house, behind the thatched grain store raised high on tall spindly legs where our maize cobs are stored each year, next to our last small tomato vine, the corner of a folded sheet of paper can just be seen. A small round gourd decorated with beads rests on top of it. Ma must have put them there. While Chibwe keeps guard, I pretend to search for unripe tomatoes, then I scoop up the paper and gourd and we run back to the ilala palms to see what we've been given.

Chibwe reads aloud from Ma's letter.

Dear Chibwe and Chipo,

> *My brave and clever children. You are right. The two of you need to run away together to a safe place. I must stay and try to keep Kambili from doing more damage to Pa and the farm.*

Tonight, Malasha, the Charcoal Burner, will wait for both of you by the baobab tree at the crossroads. He will give you a lift to the Big City. When you arrive go at once to my sister's house. Aunt Chimunya will take care of you until the drought is over.

Kambili is an evil Drought Witch who comes to stay when people don't take care of their land. We need to find a way of defeating her and that means we must ask Makemba, the Wise Woman of the Garden, to help us. The Wise Woman, Makemba, lives in the forest by the source of the Great River. It's a very long dangerous journey to reach her. You must ask Aunt Chimunya to take a message to Makemba and ask her to help us.

Tonight, I will make sure that Kambili is fast asleep and then I will come to say goodbye to you both and bring you some food for your journey.

Here is a gourd of magic herbs for Chipo to look after. You may need to use it if danger threatens you both, but do so with care.

Chibwe, keep this letter and the address of Aunt Chimunya safe, so that you can find where she lives.

Go carefully and go well my dearest children.

Your mother, Ma.

I ask Chibwe to read the letter aloud again, we talk about it then I read it once more.

"I feel better now," Chibwe says. "We know what we can do at last."

I nod and try to look pleased. I don't want to tell Chibwe that even though I'm glad to have a plan of action, I am also terrified.

"It does feel like it's going to be hard, doesn't it?" I say. "I mean it's not going to be easy – it's going to take us quite a long time to do all of this, isn't it? When will we be able to come home?"

I think I might cry again, but Chibwe gives me a serious look.

"At least we'll be together," he says. "We'll depend on each other and we'll be a team."

Chibwe looks up at the sun.

"It'll be sunset in a few hours. We need to get ready and we need to have a rest, too. It's nearly two hours' walk in the dark to the baobab tree and we must not be late to meet Malasha."

Chibwe and I both know Malasha, the Charcoal Burner, who lives alone in the forest. He cuts down trees, makes a big heap of wood, then he covers them with earth and sets fire to them. That turns the trees into charcoal. Pa asked him to come and cut down all the trees for us on one of our fields. Chibwe and I watched him work.

"We need charcoal to put in our stoves and under our pots to cook our food," Ma tells me when she is showing me how to cook maize meal. "It's our traditional way to cook when we have no electricity."

"I would rather that the trees are made into charcoal than just burnt up." Pa explained when Malasha was cutting down our trees. "I need the land cleared so I can plant a new crop there. That way the trees aren't wasted."

Ma sighed when she watched.

"In the cities there is not enough electricity, so too many people are using charcoal and that means too many trees are being chopped down. There are too many people cutting down trees who do not understand the forest as Malasha does."

"We do need to replace the trees we use," Pa agreed.

I know that Malasha smells of woodsmoke and fires and that he doesn't talk very much.

"Malasha is a hermit who lives in the forest most of the year. People say he talks to the birds in their own language and he can make them obey him," Pa said.

"Malasha is very wise about the way all the creatures in the forests live together," Ma said. "I understand plants but Malasha understands trees, birds and insects."

Chibwe and I know that he also has a big lorry that he fills up with the knobbly bags of charcoal that he sells in the Big City. What will it be like to go all that way with him?

CHAPTER SIX
MALASHA THE CHARCOAL BURNER

"How will we know when to get up and leave?" I ask Chibwe.

"I'll stay awake," he answers. "You sleep and I'll wake you up when it's time. We must go when the late moon rises but before the cocks start to crow."

"I don't know if I can sleep," I say. "I'm too hungry."

I don't say I'm afraid, because Chibwe must be too.

"Don't worry, little sister," he says. "I'll look after you."

It annoys me when Chibwe treats me as if I'm a baby just because I say what I feel. I know he has fears and worries too, but we mustn't fight, so I say nothing. The emptiness in my stomach keeps on bumping into the cold hollow place in my chest. I can't shut my eyes and they keep staring at the hot dark night even though I can't see anything. Then I hear Chibwe's breathing change and I know he's fast asleep.

"This is much too difficult for us," I think. "Let's give up trying."

That's when my eyes close at last and I drift into a dream where there is no Kambili and no drought.

Something disturbs me. There's a touch on my face.

"Wake up, Chipo. It's time to leave." Ma's hand is on my cheek and she's whispering into my ear. "Don't forget the gourd of herbs."

"Wake up, Chibwe." Ma turns to my brother and rubs his head gently. "Kambili is dozing but not for long. You must go at once."

We have almost no time to say goodbye before we're running away from the farmhouse. My heart is thudding loudly and I have to keep licking my lips and swallowing.

"Hush!" Chibwe says. "Breathe quietly!"

"You're panting too!" I say. "Can you see the road?"

The half-moon in the sky throws dark shadows beneath the trees so it's hard to see the rocks and roots under our feet and we both trip up several times. I fall over and scrape my knee. It feels sticky and hurts but I can't see what I've done to it. There are strange sounds around us that make me jump. I clutch at Chibwe's hand and he squeezes my fingers.

"It's okay," he says. "Whatever is out there in the bush will be running away from us."

There are rustles and strange calls and some twigs breaking. A huge light-coloured owl flies silently over our heads and down the path ahead of us.

"Maybe it's showing us the way. Maybe it's a friend of Malasha," I say.

Chibwe looks back over his shoulder quickly.

"Is she following us?" I ask, not wanting to turn my head.

"I can't see or hear anything behind us," he says. "We must just keep walking. We don't want to miss Malasha."

That's when I begin to worry whether we might be on the wrong path.

"It's hard to measure time in the night, isn't it?" I whisper. It doesn't feel right to speak out loud when we're in the bush at night.

"Look at the moon," Chibwe says. "It's starting to lean

towards the earth. See those stars – they have tilted over a little too. Those are our guiding stars because they always point halfway between the place where the sun rises and the sun sets. We've been walking for over an hour now so we are getting closer to the crossroads."

We feel the looming presence of the giant baobab tree even before we see its enormous white shape in front of us. We run towards it and lean against the folding curves of its huge sagging trunk. It is a friend.

"You can see this tree from a long way away," Chibwe says.

"I know," I tell him. "That's why all the roads and paths meet under it. You just have to point to it in the distance and say we'll find you at the baobab tree. Everybody knows that!"

We are quiet, listening to the night creatures all around us.

"We're not too late, are we?" I say.

"There are not new tyre marks on the road or any smell of diesel from his lorry." Chibwe scuffs the ground with his feet. "So we haven't missed him yet."

"I suppose we'll hear the lorry first?" I say.

Chibwe nods.

"I'll climb up and get us some baobab seed pods. The seeds are good to suck when you're thirsty."

It doesn't take Chibwe long to climb up the baobab because of all its bumps and knobs. He throws some of the hard velvety grey-green shuttle-shaped pods down to me and by the time he's slid down the baobab trunk again we can hear the rough uneven sound of an old lorry in the distance. I want to hide behind a tree until I know it really is Malasha but Chibwe won't let me.

"He doesn't expect us to be here. We have to be ready to wave at him and ask him for a lift."

We don't have to wave at Malasha because he stops his lorry under the baobab anyway to get out his tobacco and his pipe for a smoke. His lorry has no headlights and there is a lit oil lantern hanging off a stick over the back bumper.

"Malasha must have waited for the moon to shine before he set off in the dark," Chibwe guesses.

"I suppose that's how Ma knew when he would get to the baobab tree," I say, understanding at last.

Malasha doesn't seem surprised to see us but I remember that nothing surprised him when he was clearing the land for Pa either. He's a big man who smells of woodsmoke and his old jacket and trousers are a dusty charcoal black. His knobbly hands remind me of the burnt sticks left after a bushfire.

"Hello, Ma Chiluba's children," Malasha says. "You want to get a lift with me to the Big City, don't you?"

We both nod our heads hard. He looks us over through the smoke from his pipe.

"There's some roasted maize cobs and cans of fizzy orange in my cab. Climb in. Help yourselves."

Chibwe puts one foot on the lorry's front tyre and hauls himself into the cab by holding onto the door frame, then he helps me get in too. The lorry has no doors and there's a big hole in the cab floor. The seats have no springs and have been patched many times with old sacks. Chibwe and I grin at each other as we chew the maize cobs. Then we see who can make the loudest slurping sounds as we drink fizzy orange. I look out of the space with no door. It's a long way down to the road.

"You'd better sit between Malasha and me in case you fall asleep," Chibwe says.

"Will you be okay?" I ask and Chibwe laughs.

"Me! I'm a boy! Of course I will!"

I want to give him a push.

"You'll just have a harder fall!" I tell him.

Malasha puts his hot pipe in a jacket pocket marked with many burnt holes. The lorry engine is still thudding away. He uses both hands and shifts into a forward gear. The clutch screams, the transmission groans and we move away from the baobab tree. I want to sleep, and so does Chibwe, but it's impossible. We're banged and bumped. Even our teeth are jolted. The journey takes hours and hours. The engine strains and coughs. The lorry grinds its noisy way slowly out of the Valley, away from home, away from Ma and Pa, and away, we hope, from Kambili on the dirt track up and through the hills.

"Ow! The metal is hot!" Chibwe complains and sucks his burnt fingers.

"At least its warmer inside the lorry," I think. The night air is cooling fast

We arrive at the junction with the main city road just as the sun is rising and when I think my head will fall off with tiredness if there is another bump.

"The road will be smoother from now on till we reach the City. I'll just stop for a smoke," Malasha says.

He turns the wheel to park the lorry under a tree but as he pulls over there is a deafening noise and the lorry's engine explodes. Clouds of steam and smoke burst from the lorry and hot oil and bits of fiery metal scatter over the bushes by the roadside. Chibwe leaps out, pulling me after him into a heap on the ground. Malasha is still for a moment, then he abandons the cab with a mighty leap.

"My lorry is finished! It can't be fixed!"

He sinks down by the roadside, shakes his head and then puts it in his hands. After a moment we sit down too.

"What can we do?" Chibwe asks, but Malasha doesn't answer. All I know is that I must go to sleep.

"I'm so tired," I say, yawning. "Can't think now."

A man comes from a nearby house to see if we are hurt.

He shakes his head when he sees the lorry.

A woman brings us some water to drink.

She also shakes her head and clicks her tongue.

"Is that your father?" she asks, pointing at Malasha with her chin.

"No. He's just taking us to the Big City," Chibwe answers.

Malasha lifts his head and asks if they have a mobile phone he can borrow.

"I'll phone my brother," he says, but when his brother answers, he lowers his head again.

"He's coming to help me but he's busy now – maybe in three weeks' time!"

That's when I lie down and fall asleep by the roadside. Chibwe does the same.

PART TWO

THE CITY

CHAPTER ONE
MR WABENZI

Chibwe and I don't get to rest for very long. Even roads that are far from cities like this one have traffic that comes and goes. There are also roadside stalls where people sell things like mats, baskets and food. Most of the time there's nothing for the stallholders to do but sit and gossip. I hear bits of conversation because the ground is too hard for me to sleep properly and I don't feel safe.

"There's a bad drought in the Valley."

"Aha – that's so – this year the harvest will be poor."

"Mmm – people don't have enough food to eat."

"That's why some people are killing elephants and selling the ivory."

"That's bad! Very bad! I hear they kill rhinos as well."

"Yes – and there's stealing going on too!"

"What is there to steal from poor farmers?"

"The most valuable things of all – the ceremonial masks for the Rain Festival. They can sell them for a lot of money in Europe."

"Ah – but you can't steal the Rain Spirits!"

"That's true – but without the ceremonial masks the Spirits don't feel honoured so they don't visit the Valley and bring the rain any more."

"Careful now! There's that rich man with the Mercedes coming along the road – do you think he will stop?"

"Do you think he'll buy anything?"

"What do you think he'll pay for? All his friends are thieves and poachers."

"That's not all he does! He kidnaps . . ."

The black car that pulls up at the road junction is so quiet and smooth that it doesn't disturb Malasha. The stallholders stare at the man who gets out and talk quietly about him. Chibwe and I sit up and listen to them.

"Look at that expensive suit. Its from far away I think!"

"That's Mr Wabenzi – he goes shopping in an aeroplane!"

"Look – he has gold rings and long finger nails."

"Huh! He does no work! He has many wives perhaps!"

"Huh! He has a rich wife and many servants!"

The car has smoked-glass windows. The man's eyes are hidden behind smoked glasses. His suit is tight and shiny around his fat belly. His cheeks are tight and shiny around his fat white smile.

"Chibwe – look at his shoes!" I whisper. "They're made from the stomach skin of baby crocodiles!"

"His tie is made from real snakeskin," Chibwe whispers back.

Mr Wabenzi looks around him. His smile doesn't change. He rocks on his heels looking at the stallholders.

"What have you got for me today? Anything special? Anything new?"

He doesn't sound as if he expects a reply but the woman who asked us if Malasha was our father goes up to him and points at us.

"Those children need a lift to the Big City," she says and then she looks down at the ground.

One of Mr Wabenzi's eyebrows curves up over his dark sunglasses then disappears like a lizard's tail.

"Hello little lady," he says to me. "Hello big boy," he says to Chibwe. "Do you two both need my help? Do you want a lift to the Big City?"

Chibwe and I look at each other. We are both thinking the same thing. Is Kambili still chasing after us? Will she catch us soon? How can we get to the Big City and Aunt Chimunya? The people around us are all silent, watching us and Mr Wabenzi. Malasha lifts his head out of his hands and starts shaking it again, this time harder than ever.

"No Chibwe, no Chipo! Don't go! Wait for my brother to come. I'll take you to the City – soon!"

Nobody else speaks. Chibwe and I look down the dirt road to the Valley. We see some dust blowing up towards us. It starts to twist into a whirlwind.

"Yes please Mr Wabenzi," we say together. "Please take us to the Big City."

Someone behind us lets out their breath in a big sad sigh.

Mr Wabenzi opens the back door of his Mercedes car.

"Climb in, my dears. There's a bag of sweeties behind the driver's seat for you."

Then he turns towards the woman who told him we needed a lift and gives her a rectangular piece of stiff green paper.

"Is that money that he's giving her?" I wonder.

However, I'm already in the car. The back seat is so

comfortable and wide and there's a folded blanket on it. Chibwe has started to eat the sweets. I only want to sleep. The last thing I hear is Malasha calling out to us.

"Remember the birds, Chipo! Remember the insects, Chibwe!"

CHAPTER TWO
THE CITY MARKET

I wake up in luxury and think of home. Luxury is a new word for me. Ma and Pa told me that in our farm life there was no luxury living. Then they both laughed and told me that living in luxury means having beautiful and expensive things that nobody needs. Having such different thoughts at the same moment, first about Ma and Pa, then Mr Wabenzi's car makes me feel cut in half. I notice Chibwe is alert and sitting up very straight like the time he saw a lion near the river. He is staring out of the car window.

"What's wrong, Chibwe?" I ask.

"It's Mr Wabenzi and those people," he answers. "Something's wrong!"

The car we're in is parked next to a red building painted with tall yellow letters saying THE QUICK GET-HAPPY TARVERN AND RESTORANT. Mr Wabenzi is waving his arms at an enormous woman wearing a bright patterned dress with huge puffy sleeves and with a big-bowed turban on her head. Beside her is a shifty-looking man with a heavy gold watch on his wrist. They all turn towards the car.

"Let's get out and run!" I grab at the door.

"We're locked in," Chibwe says. "I've tried. The door works by pushing buttons."

"Where are we?" I look around for help.

"It's a market. We must have got to the Big City but I don't know where exactly. It's so busy and so big."

Chibwe and I had only seconds left together before Mr Wabenzi and the two strangers are by the car. The men reach in, take Chibwe by his arms and drag him out. The woman comes around to my side, smiles at me, opens the door, grabs me by my hair and yanks me out. I scream and she slaps my face hard with her flat hand. I see flashing lights and hear humming sounds.

"Annoy me and I'll hit you again even harder," she says with another smile. "Call me Ma Richwoman and do everything I say. My husband is Mr Badman. Show him respect!"

I nod frantically as I twist to see what is happening to Chibwe. Mr Wabenzi and Badman are taking him towards a concrete storeroom with no windows. I can see they are hurting him and every time he makes a sound, they hurt him even more. Badman unlocks the padlock on the storeroom latch and Wabenzi throws Chibwe into the room. It's dark in there but I think I see someone or something else moving. Chibwe will not be alone but is it something horrible? Badman slams the door and puts the key up high on top of the door frame. Richwoman has her heavy hand on my head and her fingers in my hair. My face is still throbbing. I cover it with my hands and peek out. Wabenzi and Badman approach us looking very pleased.

"These two should bring in good money. They look like healthy kids. Are you sure they're orphans?" Ma Richwoman says.

"They were by themselves on the road out of the Valley. Life's difficult there because of the drought. The mother of one of my poachers pointed them out to me. She knows what's good for her and her son," Mr Wabenzi replies. Then he asks, "Have you got buyers for these kids?"

Ma Richwoman nods.

"Yes. There are always bad witches who want to chop up children for rituals and there are bad doctors who want body parts. The new boy will fetch more money than that scrawny street kid we picked up."

"And the girl?" Wabenzi says poking me in the chest.

"I need help in the kitchen right now," Ma Richwoman says, giving my hair a sharp tug. "There's always a market for girl slaves though if she gives me any cheek! She can get to work at once!"

"The drought is getting much worse in the Valley," Mr Wabenzi says, looking pleased. "A bad drought really does suit me and my plans to start a copper mine there. People will starve and die or they'll leave the Valley. I'll tell the government that a copper mine will give people work and food. Yebo! The government will grant me a mining licence."

"Nothing you can do to make the drought worse, short of magic, is there?" Ma Richwoman says.

Mr Wabenzi pushes out his bottom lip and taps the side of his nose.

"Me – I'm powerful. I even have the Drought Witch, Kambili, working for me!"

CHAPTER THREE
THE GET-HAPPY TARVERN AND
RESTORANT

I know what I have to do.

I mustn't make Richwoman angry and I have to watch everyone carefully and listen to what they say. I must find out where we are and then try to understand how everything works and what everybody does. At least Richwoman doesn't have swivelling eyes like Kambili and unlike Kambili she needs a lot more sleep. All the people around Richwoman are either angry or afraid or both, but she never stops smiling even when she is being mean. All the people around Badman are either getting drunk and happy or they are already very drunk and very unhappy.

Ma Richwoman has questions for me.

"Are you and your brother orphans?" she asks.

I don't tell lies but I don't want her to know anything about me either. I nod and shake my head and try to look scared all at the same moment. Ma and Pa are too far away to help us but I don't know if Ma Richwoman can do something terrible to them as well.

"I expect they died of the AIDS disease too," she says. "There's good medicine for it now so they must have been poor and uneducated. Did they become thin and weak before they died?"

I hang my head down and look as if I'm going to cry. It's

how I feel anyway. Ma and Pa know all about how people get HIV and AIDS. Ma says that HIV/AIDS is an illness that first infected people by pure accidental chance.

"It's nobody's fault that such a disease exists," Ma told us back at home. "If you are sensible and careful you will not be infected and become ill."

Ma and Pa have taught Chibwe and me how to behave so we don't get it but I think it's better if I pretend that we were an ignorant family.

Ma Richwoman squeezes my arm and pats my stomach.

"I suppose you're too stupid to know if you and your brother have HIV/AIDS. You look healthy enough, though. There's plenty of silly people who think that the bad magic of witches will cure them of this illness."

She lets go of me and gives me a shove.

"Get on with your work!"

After that I'm much too busy to think about the dreadful fate that Ma Richwoman and Pa Badman have planned for Chibwe and me.

My main jobs are to stir the big pot of meat stew for the restaurant so that it doesn't burn and to keep the fire going so that it doesn't get cold. I also have to cook the bigger pot of maize meal for the customers. It's very hard work and takes a long time. When you start to cook the maize meal, it boils and bubbles and spits angrily. I get splashed and every splash is so hot that it burns for a long time. When the maize meal starts to stiffen and become solid enough to eat then stirring it takes a lot of effort and strength. I get very tired because the pot is almost as big as I am but Ma taught me well and Ma Richwoman is pleased with my work.

"You'll do till I find a better cook," Ma Richwoman says. "But I'm looking for a good price for you!"

There's a man in the bar who says he plans to buy me.

"He hasn't got much money and he wastes it all on beer. He can't afford you!" Ma Richwoman tells me.

Another of my jobs is keeping the back yard swept and tidy. The back yard is where the beer drinkers sit at tables under the monkey orange tree. I like the monkey orange tree because it reminds me of home. It's got big thorns, a poisonous bark and beautiful hard round yellow fruits that have a sweet tasting flesh inside. It doesn't give much shade so the beer drinkers are always thirsty. From listening to the conversations of the customers, I find out that THE QUICK GET-HAPPY TARVERN AND RESTORANT is in the Central Market of the Big City. The bus station and taxi rank are close by and that means Aunt Chimunya's house can't be very far away.

"Get two plates of food and some water for the boys in the storeroom," Pa Badman says then he goes back to the bar.

"You can take them to the boys," Ma Richwoman says.

I can hardly breathe I'm so excited at the thought that I'll see Chibwe but Ma Richwoman opens the door and stands there.

"Be quick! Not a word or else!"

She shows me the palm of her hand.

"Ma Richwoman, what is the time please?" I say loudly to her as she opens the door. I want Chibwe to hear my voice though I mustn't speak to him.

"It's 21 hours, Chipo," she replies. "You've got lots more work to do before you get to sleep."

I can't see anything in the storeroom because it's too dark. I hope Chibwe can see me. I know now there's a street kid in there with him and I hope they are able to be friends. I put the two plates of food carefully on the floor. Under one plate I was holding a book of matches I picked up under a table in the yard. On the other plate under the maize meal I have put a candle stub I found on the kitchen shelf next to the salt and pepper. I hope Chibwe and the street kid find them both in the dark. I hope the street-kid doesn't eat the candle stub by mistake.

Ma Richwoman locks me into the kitchen when she goes off to bed. Badman keeps the bar open long after that. I'm so tired I don't even cry. I just sleep until the sun rises in spite of the squeaking of mice and rats. Nothing happens and nobody comes in for quite a long time so I have time to think. I don't know how to get Chibwe out of the storeroom and I don't know what direction we should run in if we could find our way out of the market. I don't think anyone that I've seen in the bar so far would help us. Chibwe and I are both trapped and I feel helpless.

When I go into the yard there are some friendly tiptol birds around the monkey orange tree. They have yellow patches under their tails and black crests.

"Dear tiptol birds, who are friends of Malasha, bring me someone to help me please!" I say to them.

They fly away when Ma Richwoman appears with more work for me.

I'm busy collecting up all the beer bottles before lunchtime when a quite different person comes into the bar. The tiptol birds come back too. This person is young and has pleasant manners. He looks at me with interest.

"Hello. You're working hard," he says. "What's your name?"

"Good morning. I'm Chipo," I say. He reminds me of my schoolteacher.

Ma Richwoman strides over smiling even more than usual.

"Chipo's my niece. Her mother's in hospital having a baby. What can I get you? You're new around here, aren't you?"

The young man takes a step back. Ma Richwoman is wider and heavier than him.

"I've always lived around here," he says. "Please – I'll have a Coke."

Ma Richwoman brings one over to him and opens it. I carry on collecting bottles and listening.

"I'm working at the refuge for street kids," he says. "A couple of them have been missing for a few days. I was looking for them in the market."

"Terrible nuisance those street kids!" Ma Richwoman gives him a spiteful smile. "I chase them away if they come near the bar. Take those empty bottles to the kitchen, Chipo." She smacks her hands together as if she's chasing chickens. "You are a good man Mr – what's your name? I'll bring you a beer."

"I'm David Lengwe – thank you – but I don't want a beer."

Ma Richwoman fetches a beer from the bar then follows me into the kitchen where she opens it. I see her pick up a box of powder from the floor. I know its rat poison because I read the label this morning. Richwoman turns her back to block me from seeing that she is pouring some of it into the beer but I have ears. I hear the beer fizz. When that stops, she carries it out to David Lengwe.

"Go and wipe the tables my darling Chipo," she says so that David Lengwe will hear her. "And clean the ashtrays."

What am I going to do? Ma Richwoman doesn't care if I know that she is poisoning David Lengwe. If I warn him, she'll beat me or sell me and what will she do to Chibwe? I'm in her power. It's safer for me to do nothing but if I do nothing, I'll have helped kill him and I'll be as bad as she is. I wipe the tables with the dirty cloth from the kitchen and keep watching him. Ma Richwoman comes up behind me and puts her hand on my head and her fingers in my hair. I'm facing David Lengwe.

"Enjoy your beer, Mr Lengwe!" she says.

David Lengwe smiles at her and lifts his beer bottle. He can see me looking at him. I make a terrible face, roll my eyes, stick my tongue out and try to look as if I'm choking. David Lengwe looks puzzled but still smiles. He puts the bottle down. I stop pulling faces. He picks the bottle up again and I pull my dying face again. The bottle goes down again once more. Ma Richwoman is suspicious.

"Chipo! Get on with your work!" She gives me such a hard shove that I fall over.

David Lengwe leaps up to help me and knocks the beer bottle over. The split beer sizzles and steams. It leaves a pink stain on the table. David Lengwe looks at the stain. He's shocked, but not I think, surprised. His expression hardens.

"I'll bring you another beer. That one looks bad!" Ma Richwoman says.

"Thanks so much – but I have to get back to work," he says. "That Chipo's a good worker. Take care of her, won't you. I'll be back tonight."

Richwoman gives my hair a sharp tug. She's annoyed that she hasn't succeeded in poisoning David Lengwe, but she's distracted by more customers demanding drinks.

"Get on with cleaning. There's lunch to be cooked."

I'm so relieved. David Lengwe didn't get poisoned and I didn't get beaten. If I was to poison Ma Richwoman and Badman with rat poison, then Chibwe and I might be able to escape, but I don't want to kill anyone. Then I remember the gourd of herbs that Ma gave me. I know what some of the herbs can do but I'll have to plan when exactly to use them. Last night Ma Richwoman and Badman ate their supper together before the bar got too busy. They kept the best meat for themselves. I wonder if they'll have their food at the same time tonight.

I work at the same tasks as I did the day before. It's easier because I know what to expect but its harder because I'm much more tired. The lunchtime customers have left and the evening customers haven't yet arrived. Richwoman takes out two enormous steaks from the fridge.

"Grill these for me Chipo. Mr Badman and I'll have green relish and maize meal with them."

"Yes Ma Richwoman," I say.

My heart is racing. This is the moment to see what Ma's herbs will do. I do my best to make the meat and relish as delicious as possible. When it's almost ready and when Ma Richwoman and Badman are sitting down waiting to be served, I secretly sprinkle Ma's herbs into the relish and stir them in. If anything, the relish smells even better. It makes me feel hungry but I manage to stop myself from tasting it.

"Mm. This smells good!" says Badman.

"Mm. I'm starving!" says Ma Richwoman and they both start to gobble up their food.

I bring them more beers, and then some more beers. Soon they are laughing uproariously, banging on the table, and talking louder and louder. The noisier they get, the noisier the customers get too. I was hoping that they would both want to go to sleep. I didn't expect this. Then the mood starts to change. Ma Richwoman and Badman begin to laugh at their customers and call them names.

"You are stupid people!"

"All you do is drink!"

"We are stealing from you all the time!"

"You don't know that we are doing it!"

"Idiots!"

In a very short time, everybody begins to fight with everybody else. Chairs are thrown about and tables broken. I find a safe corner to hide in. The police are on duty in the market at night. Somebody calls them and then there is more fighting until at last Ma Richwoman and Badman are arrested for brawling and the bar is cleared.

Now is my chance to free Chibwe. I sweep the storeroom key off the top of the door frame with a long broom. The padlock is still too high for me to reach. As I turn around to look for a chair to stand on that isn't broken somebody comes up behind me and grabs my wrist. I scream.

CHAPTER FOUR
DAVID LENGWE

"What are you doing? Can I help? I saw that there was a fight in the bar and that the police were here."

It's David Lengwe. I'm so relieved that I start to cry.

"Please – my brother is locked in the storeroom. Help me get him out!"

In a minute David has opened the storeroom and Chibwe and the street kid stumble out blinking into the bright lights of the bar. They are dirty and smelly and afraid. I throw my arms around my brother and we both cry and smile at each other. The streetkid looks around nervously and then tries to run past us. But David Lengwe catches his arm.

"Hey, Masika! What are you doing here? It's alright! What happened to you? You're safe now."

"Who's that?" Chibwe asks me looking at David.

"He's okay," I say and then add, "I think so."

David laughs.

"Your sister saved me from being very sick – I'm in her debt – but Masika knows me. I'm David."

The street kid Masika nods. He is already holding tight to David's hand.

"I think we need to get you all somewhere safe and then you can tell me why you're here."

"You must look in this storeroom first, David." Chibwe says. "The stuff in there belongs to Mr Wabenzi."

David finds an outside light switch, looks into the storeroom and exclaims in surprise.

"Wow! Mr Wabenzi hey! Its even more important we go somewhere really safe as fast as possible. Follow me!"

We race outside looking around to see who's watching us. David has an old car parked close by and we all climb in and he drives away as quickly as he can. I don't know where I am or which direction our home in the Valley is or in which direction Aunt Chimunya lives. I have no idea where anyone would have to go to find Makemba and the Source of the Great River. I don't think Chibwe knows where he is either and I'm sure that Masika has never been in a car before. He has made his legs and arms all stiff but his eyes are shut, there's a big scared smile on his face and we're not even going very fast.

David pulls the car over into a quiet street away from the market and we all start talking at once trying to explain what has happened to us. Masika says that he was tricked into accepting food from Badman and then made a prisoner.

"We all know that those people sell us to witches who chop up street kids like me and use us for bad medicine," he says.

"It could have happened to us as well," Chibwe says, then he turns to me with a question.

"Chipo – what did happen to make Badman and Richwoman get arrested? You were there – what happened?" Chibwe sees my face. "Chipo – you must tell us. Did you do something?"

"It was Ma's herbs," I say and then I explain what happened.

"You're a clever girl!" David says smiling. "Well done!"

Masika and Chibwe both hug me. I think that I'm probably

as smelly as them anyway with all my work in Ma Richwoman's dirty kitchen.

"We need to think this through very carefully," David says with a frown. "You say those things in the storeroom belong to Mr Wabenzi, Chibwe? I do know that Richwoman and Badman work for him. Wabenzi has friends in government and in the police so they will soon be out of the police cells and they won't be charged with fighting or even fined. If they think that you are all orphans without any family, they won't hurry to get you back, but they won't give up looking for you either. We have to think where Masika can hide away safely. Chipo, you and Chibwe will be safe with your aunt or you can go home to the Valley. What is most dangerous for you all is that you know what was hidden in the storeroom. That puts all your lives in danger. Mine too, if they think I was there as well and saw it all."

"What was hidden there?" I ask impatiently. "I couldn't see into that dark room and next minute we were all running away."

"We saw everything," Chibwe explains. "That candle and matches you gave us meant that we could see them."

"I was afraid!" Masika shudders at the memory. "Of the Spirits!"

"There were elephant tusks, and the teeth and horns from other animals and then there were the Ritual Masks and the costumes for the dancers and some drums too," Chibwe continues.

"Oh!"

That's all I say because it is such a serious matter for all our lives if the Spirits and the Shades of the Ancestors are offended.

"Let's take you to your Aunt Chimunya," David says. "I'll look after Masika."

"Aren't you the first person that Badman and Richwoman will visit when they look for him?" Chibwe asks.

"Yes," says David simply. "I'll find a way to hide Masika."

He turns to us.

"Chipo and Chibwe, I want to know why ever did the two of you leave home all by yourselves and come to the Big City? It's such a long dangerous journey for you!"

Chibwe and I look at each other with sighs of relief. At last we are safe.

Chibwe explains.

"We were supposed to have a lift all the way here with our friend, the charcoal burner, Malasha. Ma told us to come to ask her sister, Aunt Chimunya, for help. We need Aunt Chimunya to make the journey for us to the Source of the Great River to ask the Wise Woman Makemba to break the dry spell that the Drought Witch has put on our farm in the Valley."

"That's another long dangerous journey," David says. "It's better if your Aunt goes all that way for you."

"Yes, it is much better!" Chibwe and I say together and we smile at each other.

"We'll be able to go home soon!" Chibwe says.

"The worst is over for you two, then! That's good!" David says. "And I'll find somewhere safe for Masika. Let's phone Aunt Chimunya now."

CHAPTER FIVE
AUNT CHIMUNYA'S DAUGHTER.

Ma had given us Aunt Chimunya's mobile phone number so David calls her to say that Chibwe and I are coming to stay with her for a while.

"They've had a terrible time here in the Big City," he says. "They'll tell you all about it when we get to your house."

"Get to my house? Coming to stay? What's happened to my sister Chiluba and her husband Mulenga? I've had such bad feelings! I know something isn't right. Staying with me? Ah – yes – that's – okay – I think!"

David frowns as he listens to her.

"Is your aunt well? She sounds rather confused and flustered. Is she expecting you?"

"She's fine!" I say trying to sound confident. "She's Ma's sister."

Chibwe yawns and agrees. "Aunt Chimunya and Ma are very close. They always know what each other is thinking."

A little worm of worry starts to chew away inside me.

"Did they know this time?"

David sounds the car horn when we arrive at the house and the security gate jerks, then rumbles open. He parks by the front door and Aunt Chimunya runs out to give Chibwe and me a hug.

"How lovely to see you both – my word, you are dirty, Chipo, and you smell, Chibwe! What's happened to you both? Where are your mother and father? Are they coming too? Who is this man?" Aunt Chimunya looks at David who has got out of the car to greet her. Masika is fast asleep on the car's back seat.

"Ah!" she says recognising him with surprise. "I know you! You're the one who works with the street kids and AIDS orphans in town." And Aunt Chimunya starts to cry.

"We are a house in mourning," she says. "My son-in-law has died from this same dreadful AIDS a few days ago and my daughter is ill with HIV. I'm nursing her and looking after all of her children."

"I'm so sorry to hear that," David says. "Can I help in any way?"

"We have a good doctor," Aunt Chimunya says. "We have the medicine we need for my daughter. She will be all right and the children are all healthy. The house is so full." She looks at Chibwe and me.

"Oh – you poor things. You need to eat and you need to have a shower right away. We'll talk in the morning. You'll have to sleep on the settees in the sitting room tonight. Come on in all of you."

David says that he must go and I hear my aunt ask him quietly if something terrible has happened to her sister and her brother-in-law?

"No, it's not HIV or AIDS," David says. "There's a serious drought in the Valley. The children will explain it to you. Masika also wants to be washed and fed when I get home – if I can wake him up. I must go."

He calls out to us with a smile, "Take care, Chipo and Chibwe. We'll meet again. If you need me you can phone."

I don't want to say goodbye to David.

"Thank you for saving us both!" I tell him.

"Chipo, you saved me, didn't you? We'll stay friends and we won't forget each other."

Aunt Chimunya's home is bright and clean. It's not very big but it is noisy. The television is on and there are three small wide-eyed children sitting in front of it on the settee. They turn to look at us.

The oldest boy is six years old. He holds his hand in front of his face and wrinkles his nose.

"Why are you so dirty?" he asks.

The two younger children copy his expression but then turn back to watch the television.

"Don't be rude, Simon," Aunt Chimunya says and she takes Chibwe and me to the shower so we can take it in turns to wash.

"When you're clean, go to the dining room and my maid will give you some supper," Aunt Chimunya says. "I must go and see to Faith, my daughter. It's time for her medicines."

Chibwe and I are alone while we eat. At first we concentrate on our plates of food. After we've scraped them clean, we talk.

"This is bad news," Chibwe says. "I didn't know cousin Faith and her husband were ill."

"Ma and Pa never said anything. Perhaps they didn't know either?" I answer. "They told us about AIDS. So did our teacher."

"They would have told us if they knew about Faith," Chibwe says.

We were told it was important to finish our schooling and we were taught that men and women had to respect each other and take care of each other with loving and having sex. Remembering our teacher at this moment makes the Valley, the farm and the school seem so far away. I wonder if Kambili's arrival in a dust storm and her enchantment of Pa did really happen. Maybe it's only a bad dream from a long time ago.

"I'm so tired – I want to go to bed now – tomorrow we'll do it," I say.

I know there's something important that has to be done soon.

"I don't think that Aunt Chimunya can go to the Rainforest to find the wise woman Makemba when she has to look after her sick daughter," Chibwe says. "Do you, Chipo?"

I don't answer, instead all I hear is Aunt Chimunya's maid clicking her tongue because my head is on the table and I've fallen asleep.

CHAPTER SIX
FAITH'S CHILDREN

When Aunt Chimunya's maid comes in early the next day to get breakfast ready, she leaves us to sleep on the settee but cousin Faith's children aren't so kind. They all get up early and are so curious about us that they come into the sitting room and stand in a line in front of the settee where we are sleeping. Simon tells us he wants us to wake up so that he can talk to us. When we don't answer he pinches Chibwe's arm.

"Where are you from?"

"Why are you here?"

"What are you going to do?"

"When are you going to get up?"

"Did you know my Mummy's sick?"

"Did you know my Daddy has died?"

The youngest child asks the last question and starts to cry. Though Chibwe thinks he is strong and tough, his heart is as soft as the inside of a banana.

"Come on little Mwana, sit on my knee. Don't cry!" Chibwe smooths the child's tears away with his hand and rocks him for a moment.

"We'll go into the garden and look for some guavas to eat. Would you like that?"

He gets up and leads the three children outside to look for the guava tree. I hope there is one in the garden with fruit. It's too early for ripe mangoes. I turn my back on the room and snuggle into a cushion. I want to go back to sleep but instead Chibwe's last words yesterday come back into my brain and bang about like a bag of stones.

"Aunt Chimunya can't leave cousin Faith who is sick and her three grandchildren and go on a long journey to help Ma and Pa."

I put the cushion over my head but the words won't go away. If Aunt Chimunya can't go who else can go? Can Malasha go instead? Could we ask David? I start to feel ill myself. It's not fair. It's wrong. Can't we just go home? Maybe Kambili will have gone away by now. Maybe it was only a dream after all.

The maid comes back into the room. When she sees I'm awake she puts on the television. It's the morning news report and the news presenter is talking about the drought in the Valley, I sit up and watch. The film shows bare brown earth with a few shrivelled maize plants sticking up out of the dust then the dust lifts, blows and circles into a whirlwind. I think eyes are looking at me from out of its centre.

"There have been a lot of dust storms in the Valley," the presenter says. "People are hungry. Villagers are ill from the lack of food. See how thin some people are." The camera moves over the village near us and I recognise some of the villagers.

"We visited a farmer. This is what he said."

There on the television screen I see a picture of Pa. His eyes look unfocused and he keeps on saying over and over again,

"We can't grow anything without water. We need to take care of our land."

Standing on one side of him is Ma. She looks very tired. Kambili is there also and she is still holding onto Pa's shoulder. I think she seems fatter and more solid than before. I run outside.

"Chibwe! I've seen pictures from home on the TV! Come!"

The news is over when Chibwe comes back into the room. They don't show the same pictures at lunchtime. Instead they show a conference room in a big hotel. Mr Wabenzi is there being interviewed. He smiles and smiles at the camera.

"What the people of the Valley need to help them survive the drought, is development. We need to start mining in the Valley. That will make us rich."

"What about our natural resources? What about the farming communities? What about the people? What about our wildlife?" the interviewer asks. "Will it make you rich also?"

"I only care about the people in the Valley," Mr Wabenzi lies. "Let me introduce you to my business associate from Britain, Mr Willie Waffell. He will bring investment into the country."

He turns smiling always to a man whose hair looks like the yellow silky tassels from the top of a maize plant. He is floppier and flabbier than Mr Wabenzi, his grin is even greedier than Mr Wabenzi's, and his skin colour changes from white to pink to red as he speaks. Chibwe and I can't understand what he is saying. His speech sounds like his name and all his words run together.

"We will waffell wonderfully in the walley and will waffell it well into wealthy waffelly wich wichness and thuckseth for uth! Yeth!"

Chibwe frowns as he concentrates on the story about Mr Wabenzi and Mr Waffell on the television. He also listens carefully when I tell him what I saw.

"We need to think hard about all of this," he says. "We have to decide what the best thing to do will be. It won't be easy."

"Do you believe me?" I ask him.

"You always tell the truth, Chipo," Chibwe says.

"I think maybe I dreamed it all," I say. "Maybe it's in my imagination and not real."

"You're like Ma more than I am," he says. "I think that the Spirits talk to you more than to me. They may not seem to be real in the same way but they are just as important as things that have bodies."

That's another thing I love about Chibwe. He is so sensible about Spirits.

"What are we really going to do then?" I ask him.

"I don't know," he says. "We'll have to ask Aunt Chimunya to explain to us how to get to the Evergreen Forest on our own."

"We'll ask her tonight," I say, feeling happier again and both Chibwe and I spend the rest of the day with the children finding games to play and things to amuse them. The two smallest children don't really understand what has happened, but they both miss their mother.

"Daddy had to go away every week to work," Simon says. "He got sick when it was my birthday. I was five then." His eyes shift miserably away from the game we are playing. "Is Mummy going to get better?" he asks Chibwe.

"Oh yes!" Chibwe sounds confident. "That's what your Grandmother says. She'll be fine. The doctor has given her good medicine. Now you must be brave. Come and play with your brothers!"

Aunt Chimunya comes to us after the little children have had their supper and are watching television again.

"Thank you Chibwe and Chipo for looking after the children so well. That made my day much easier! I've had a bit more time – so now come and tell me all your news. What's this I hear about the drought in the Valley? How is my sister?"

We tell Aunt Chimunya everything, sometimes taking it in turns and sometimes speaking at the same moment. We end by telling her about Mr Wabenzi and Ma Richwoman and Pa Badman. For a while she sits in silence then she puts her arms around us and pulls us into a big hug.

"You are sensible children so you already know that I can't leave my daughter and her children until my daughter is much better. I'll try and think of someone we can trust who can go to the Evergreen Forest instead of me. It's a very long way and it isn't possible to go all the way on foot or by road so it will take weeks and maybe months to get there. Some of the journey is dangerous and, of course, no one knows if Makemba will help you, even if you can find her.

"For the moment you must stay away from the city centre where Mr Wabenzi works. He is a man who has too much power and who wants even more. He is not going to let children like you get in his way! Be very careful while you are here! He is very dangerous."

Chibwe and I nod our heads. We do know that it's all a very serious business.

"Aunt Chimunya, please tell me how to get to the Evergreen Forest and where to find Makemba," Chibwe asks.

Aunt Chimunya looks straight at him and says nothing.

"Just so that I understand how hard it is. I might be able to find somebody else who can go," Chibwe adds quickly.

"Hmmph!" Aunt Chimunya says. "Well! I will tell you so you realise that it's not a journey for children on their own."

We sit down in front of Aunt Chimunya in the dining room.

"You are not to go to the Evergreen Forest alone!" Aunt Chimunya says. "Your parents would never forgive me if I let you go – I forbid you to think of it for these reasons -

- You might be kidnapped again.
- Mr Wabenzi will still be chasing you and he might catch you.
- You need money for the bus journey to the Great River.
- You have to find a boatman to take you up the Great River.
- You need money for the boatman.
- You have to find a guide to take you to the Evergreen Forest
- You need money for the guide.
- Nobody knows where to find Makemba.
- Money can't buy a map to where Makemba lives.
- If Makemba finds you she may help you and she may not.
- Makemba probably won't help two small children."

Aunt Chimunya's list of why-nots goes on and on. After we've listened for a long time I feel as if I am held down in my chair by a great weight, but Chibwe can't stop wiggling and won't look Aunt Chimunya in the face. Aunt Chimunya decides that she's said enough.

"You can go out and play, Chibwe and Chipo. I can see that you are bored but you must understand why you can't go to the Evergreen Forest on your own! It's enough that you are in danger from Mr Wabenzi. If you disappear, I'll think he's kidnapped you. I'll get the police and go straight to Mr Wabenzi. I'll get you back!"

CHAPTER SEVEN
Masika

Chibwe and I spend the next few days helping Aunt Chimunya by looking after Faith's children and watching television. We don't have television on our farm or in the nearby village in the Valley so we find it very interesting and we enjoy ourselves. Simon explains what the different programmes are about but some of it make my head ache. Aunt Chimunya's maid is a very good cook and we eat lots of meat as well as new vegetables we haven't seen before. We're allowed to eat ice-cream every day if we want it. Aunt Chimunya keeps trying to phone the village headman or one of her distant family in the Valley to ask for news of Ma and Pa but she can't get through to anybody at all.

"Don't worry," she says. "I'll keep on trying."

I notice that Chibwe is fidgeting all the time. He keeps going to the gate and looking up and down the road, then he comes back frowning. I wonder what he's thinking. It starts to worry me.

"Chibwe, I know that you're planning something," I say to him one day. "You're not thinking of going to the Evergreen Forest without me, are you? I'll never forgive you if you do!"

Chibwe sighs and then grins.

"It's better if I go by myself. You can help Aunt Chimunya with the children. Perhaps even go back to the Valley. It's not a good idea to put both of us in danger."

"We'll be safer together!" I say firmly. "You yourself said that I'm more in touch with the Spirits than you are. That means that you can't do it without me – can you?"

"I'd like your company, Chipo," he says. "I can't forget that you saved me from being sold to a witch!"

"We're going together. That's decided!" I say. "But when?"

Chibwe shrugs and pulls a face. Neither of us know what to do or when to do it.

A car sounds its hooter at the gate. Chibwe pushes the button to open it and David Lengwe drives in.

"Is Masika here?" he asks. "He's run away from my house – at least I think he has. I'm worried that he's been kidnapped again."

"We haven't seen him," we both say. "What do you think has happened?" Chibwe asks.

"Why would he run away?" I ask.

David sighs.

"Masika's parents are also from the same Valley as your parents but like your cousin's husband they both died of AIDS. Masika is an orphan living on the streets, he's hungry, he sniffs glue. He's learnt not to trust anybody and he's afraid all the time. He thinks Badman and Richwoman will catch him soon so he's probably hiding somewhere.

"Perhaps you can help me? I'm going to drive around the city looking at all the places he might be and a couple of sharp-eyed kids like you might see him before me. If we find him, he might also listen to you two after what you all went through together."

"Sure, David," Chibwe says, climbing into the car.

"I'll tell Aunt Chimunya," I say.

We head off into town in David's car. Chibwe's bagged the front seat so I amuse myself by looking out the back window. That way I see things from a different angle.

"We won't go to the big City Market. There's no way Masika will go near Richwoman's bar," David says. "There's plenty of other small markets and supermarkets where street kids hang around begging for money or scraps of food."

"There are ever so many beggars and street kids," I say. "David, how do they keep warm at night? How can they make fires when there are no trees and no wood to burn?"

"They make fires from plastic rubbish," David says. "It's poisonous to breath the smoke from the fire and the plastic causes bad burns to their skin."

"That's terrible!" Chibwe says. "Why don't they use charcoal?"

"It's too expensive in the city," David explains. "All the trees around the city have been cut down and very poor people cook on fires made from old car tyres."

"That smells horrible!" Chibwe says wrinkling his nose.

We drive around for hours but don't see Masika. We do learn about the city though, and Chibwe asks David questions about how to get to the Evergreen Forest and which minibus goes in that direction. David gives Chibwe a hard stare after the minibus question.

"Chibwe, you mustn't go to the Evergreen Forest on your own. I'll show you on a map where it is and then you'll understand why."

David takes us back to his house and gives us some bread and sausage to eat. He pulls a map off a shelf and shows us where the Evergreen Forest is and where the Source of the Great River might be. It's a small map that shows the whole of our country and some of its main roads. David points to our home.

"Your home is a day's journey away by car or bus." He explains. "It's many days by foot."

He points to the Evergreen Forest in the opposite direction.

"The Evergreen Forest is much more than two days away. No one is sure where the source of the Great River is in the Evergreen Forest. There are no roads that go there. There are no signs and no paths through the Evergreen Forest and that's not the only difficulty. If you take a minibus from here to the Small Town on the Great River that's at least a day's travelling. From the Small Town on the Great River you can only go the rest of the way by boat. You may not even find a boatman who will take you on such a long hard journey."

I see that Chibwe looks discouraged.

"Aunt Chimunya said she would go to the Evergreen Forest if Faith wasn't sick," I say. "If she can do it why can't we?"

David shakes his head.

"I don't know. Perhaps Aunt Chimunya has friends on the Great River? Perhaps she even has special powers? I think she's an ordinary person and it would be as difficult for her as for you. She is an adult though, and now you both know how dangerous it can be for children on their own."

Chibwe is silent. I can almost hear what he's thinking and

I'm probably thinking the same thoughts as him. I'm wondering what it costs to pay for the minibus ticket and how we can earn some money.

After lunch we set off again to look for Masika and this time we drive through the city centre.

"Those buildings are very tall," Chibwe says. "Look Chipo, there's something like a car going up the side of that building!"

"Are they made of plastic?" I ask. "They're so smooth and shiny."

I think of Kambili.

"That's an elevator for carrying people to the top of the skyscraper, Chibwe," David says. "And no Chipo. The buildings are mostly made from steel, glass and concrete."

"There's one last place that I can think of where we can look for Masika," David says. "I can't do it without your help. It's a big enclosed area that we will need to search on foot. When the Big City was still new there was a small airfield right in the middle of it. It's been walled off and is now completely overgrown but sometimes street children hide away there. Mr Wabenzi plans to buy it and turn it into a factory and shops. So far he hasn't been given permission and nobody else goes there any more."

David turns his car away from the shops and houses onto a narrow grassy track and parks it under an old fig tree. A little further on we find a gap where the wall and fence have been damaged and we bend down and scramble through it.

"You both go around that way," David says pointing. "I'll go the other way. When we meet we walk through the middle together. Better call out Masika's name so he knows it's us, otherwise he'll hide and we'll never find him."

Chibwe and I fight our way through the bushes, the tall trees, and the long grass that has grown up all over the old airfield. Some of it is thorny and most of it is scratchy. There are buzzing insects, and irritating flies, lizards whizz off when we approach and the birds stop singing until we've gone past them. As we go we call out "Masika" and we whistle. We can hear David calling from the opposite side to us. Almost halfway round I trip over a wire noose made to trap small creatures. My foot is caught by it. Chibwe tugs the wire free and loosens it for me.

"There must be a mongoose here or cane rats," he says. "I wonder who made this trap? They're cruel ways to catch animals."

We don't find Masika and when we reach each other, David hasn't found him either.

"It's only to be expected," he says.

There's a heap of plastic bags and bottles glittering by the main gate. They make me think of Kambili once again.

"It's a pity that people use this place to dump their rubbish in," David says with a sigh. "It could be a recreation park."

Together we set off across the centre of the plot towards the gap in the fence.

"Look! Isn't that pretty!" I exclaim. We've come across a dip full of water in the middle of the old runway. As we come closer a flock of white egrets flap their way up from the water and circle over to some trees where they settle and wait for us leave them alone again.

"Look!" I say again. "There are some of those herbs that Ma used to pick for us when we were ill. I'll take some home for Aunt Chimunya to give to Faith."

It is so pleasant to be in a place that is full of the wild plants, trees and flowers that we knew in our Valley before the Drought Witch arrived. My arms are full by the time we reach the gap and there waiting for us is Masika.

"I'm hungry!" he says.

CHAPTER EIGHT
THE SECRET WILDERNESS

Masika refuses to leave his secret wilderness, so instead we fetch food and water for him from a nearby shop. We also bring him a big cardboard box and some plastic bags so he can fix himself somewhere dry to sleep.

"I'll come back with a blanket," David says. "I want to see you, Masika, every time I come back here – do you promise?"

Masika still won't answer. He chews the food we brought and looks at the ground. I can see David is annoyed but he knows Masika is too scared to agree.

"Okay," he says, "I'll hide food and a blanket here by the wall. I'd like to see you, though."

"We'll come and see you Masika. How's that?" Chibwe acts as if he's Masika's big brother and Masika smiles at him. I roll my eyes.

"Would you both come back and see Masika?" David looks relieved at the idea.

"Sure. We can walk here from Aunt Chimunya's house," Chibwe says.

"Don't let anyone follow you. Be careful, won't you?" David is smiling at us. I tug at David's arm.

"What about when it's dark?" I say.

"Here Masika – have these matches. Only make a small fire." David digs in his pocket for his matches. "At least in here Masika, you can burn sticks and wood. You don't have to make a fire from plastic rubbish and breathe in the poison as you and your friends do on the streets."

At last Masika speaks.

"Cigarettes," he says and holds out his hand to David.

"Smoking is bad for you," Chibwe says. I roll my eyes again. I've seen Chibwe trying to make his own cigarettes when Pa is not around.

"We'll see you tomorrow, Masika," I say.

David gives Masika the last two cigarettes in his pack.

***

Aunt Chimunya was delighted with the herbs I'd gathered for her from inside Masika's secret wilderness.

"Where did you get these? These are just right for reducing fever if I put them in a drink – and these give off a lovely scent if I burn them – they stop headaches and make it easy to breathe. Faith will be pleased! Your mother has taught you well, Chipo. Can you get me some more please?"

I tell Aunt Chimunya about Masika and his hideout.

"Poor child!" she says. "You must be very careful when you visit him. That sounds like a place where bad people hide out as well as street kids. If you and Chibwe help me with my grandchildren in the morning, I'll give you some food to take to Masika at lunch time."

"I've had an idea," I say to Chibwe as we walk to the secret wilderness to find Masika the next afternoon. "If I pick a big bunch of herbs, perhaps we can sell the ones Faith doesn't need to get some money."

Chibwe puts his head on one side as he looks at me.

"Money? You mean so we can buy a ticket for the minibus journey, Chipo? That's a very good idea but herbs aren't going to make a lot of money, are they?"

I feel very disappointed that my idea is no good but Chibwe is pulling his thinking face like he does at school, so I wait.

"I've seen women collect plastic bottles and sell them. We can collect the plastic bottles that have been left in the wilderness too. Maybe there are other things like bush fruit, that we can find in that place and also sell," he says and he turns to look at me.

"There are!" I answer. "I saw lots of fruits!"

"Do you think Masika knows about them?" Chibwe asks. "Perhaps he needs them? Perhaps he's eaten them all, anyway?"

"He's been in the city all his life. Maybe he doesn't know where to look for bush fruits?" I say.

"We'd better teach him, then," Chibwe says. "Now we've got lots of things to do if we're going to try and get to the Evergreen Forest."

"Do you think Aunt Chimunya will let us go by ourselves?" I ask.

Chibwe doesn't answer. We both know she'll will stop us if she can.

"We shouldn't worry her," I say.

We are very busy every day after that. First of all, we look after Simon and his little sisters, then we take some food and water to Masika. He doesn't hide from us when David isn't there and he talks all the time and sometimes laughs. Chibwe helps him make a tent that he can sleep in that's dry. Masika says he has to have somewhere secret to hide.

"Sometimes thieves come in to hide the things they've stolen. Once there was a homeless man who was angry and kept shouting all night. I was scared of him! Another man came in to set a trap for the guinea fowl but there are not any left now."

He show us a hole in the ground that is big enough for someone as small as him to crawl into when he's afraid. We put some dead branches around it so no one can find it.

"It looks like an anteater made it long ago" Chibwe says. Masika doesn't know what kind of animal that is.

"An anteater eats termites with its long tongue. It has a long snout and big claws and digs holes in anthills," Chibwe explains.

"I think it's my friend." Masika says. "Maybe it's my family!"

"We'll call you Wanyanga the Anteater then instead of Masika," we say, laughing.

Together we collect herbs that I can sell. We find a few tomatoes and some paw-paws growing by the broken-down airport sentry hut.

I find some tamarind pods and some of the bush fruit that people eat when they have no food left.

"It hurts your tummy to eat some bush-fruits," I tell Masika "but they have vitamins that are good for you."

Masika gives us advice about where to go to sell our herbs and fruit.

"Go to the big store where people shop who have lots of

money. Poorer people are kinder but there are rich people who like to show how generous they are when they give money to the street kids. Let Chipo sell the food. People buy more from girls than from boys, Chibwe, you must stay close by her, because some other street kids will steal from a girl if they can."

"If the shopkeeper comes out, run away fast. He doesn't like street kids selling stuff or begging outside his shop."

Masika won't leave the secret wilderness to come with us. The idea makes him dumb and he shakes his head.

"Wabenzi, no!" he says. "Wabenzi, bad Spirits!"

I don't like saying goodbye to Masika and leaving him alone at night. I understand his fear of bad Spirits because I know that Kambili is a bad spirit.

"If he feels safer staying in this little wilderness, there isn't anything we can do," Chibwe says.

Just before we leave Masika gives us some advice.

"I have a friend called William Mukuka who begs at the shops. He used to look after me. Tell him what happened to me and why I'm hiding here. He'll help you."

We get quite good at selling the few things we find in the wilderness. We know how to dodge the shopkeeper and the security guards. We learn which of the street kids will steal from us and which will leave us alone. We find Masika's friend, William Mukuka, and tell him what happened to the three of us. William is so skinny and ragged that he looks younger than he says he is but his voice is croaky and he has big teeth.

"We know about Mr Wabenzi on the street," William says. "I told Masika to be careful but he was very hungry on the day he was kidnapped. It's good you all escaped. I'll look after you two now. Mr Wabenzi has spies everywhere."

William does look out for us and he lets us keep all the money we make if we give him some of Aunt Chimunya's food and bread.

Soon we have a couple of favourite customers who find the herbs I'm selling very interesting or who say that it reminds them of their grandmother in the village. One of Aunt Chimunya's friends comes to the store but we manage to duck behind a parked car before she can see and recognise us. We aren't making much money.

"We've got enough for one of us to go half-way." Chibwe says, frowning. "This way we'll be here for a year before we can save enough."

"At least we go home to supper and a clean bed," I think.

It's still true, however. We will never be able to get enough money to go to the Evergreen Forest and find Makemba. We can't help Pa and Ma like this. I'm so sad. What about the Spirits that Chibwe says are connected to me? I need their help and I don't know how ask them for it. As I fall asleep, I wonder what it was that Malasha said to us on the roadside.

"Remember the birds! Remember the insects! Remember!"

CHAPTER NINE
WABENZI'S PLANS

We arrive at the secret wilderness carrying Masika's food and water. The day is bright and sunny again. There was a little rain last night but Masika will have been kept dry in his shelter so we aren't worried. He isn't waiting for us by the hole in the fence, though, and when we get to his sleeping place he isn't there either. I'm about to call out to him when Chibwe grabs my arm and pulls me down behind a bush.

"Shush Chipo! The big gate's open on the other side. Someone is inside here! Listen!"

I feel as if I've sat down in an ant's nest because my skin starts to crawl. I can hear voices. Chibwe and I look at each other.

"Do you think Mr Wabenzi has come here to start his building plans?" I whisper. "Do you think they've come here to kidnap Masika?"

Chibwe shakes his head.

"Listen! I think one of the voices belongs to someone who is a stranger from another country. Can you understand what they're saying?"

I close my eyes to concentrate.

"There is a woman. Her voice sounds foreign to me but there is a man who sounds as if he is from here. They are moving slowly and they are talking quietly to each other and they stop a lot and wait for the birds to sing again."

Chibwe nods. "You're right. They sound like the people who come to watch birds in the Valley. I think they've stopped by the pool of the mazira – the white egrets."

We don't have to speak to each other, we know what we are doing. We edge forward carefully until we can see the two people, a man and a woman, who are now squatting down near the pool in the shade.

"This is a unique place, Isaac." the woman says. "You do have to succeed in saving it from having houses built all over it. It will be a green lung in the city – a natural reserve for local people to visit and walk around and schoolchildren will use it as a resource for their science and ecology classes. It's so important for people to understand that without trees there is no air for people to breathe."

I know what a lung is but I've never heard of a green one. We live near the National Park so we do both know about saving wild animals and protecting plants, and natural reserves and ecology.

"That Mr Wabenzi is a problem and a dangerous opponent of our plan but I do have a powerful friend in the government," Isaac says. "When you have finished your report, Palma, on all the different species of plants and trees that grow on this plot, and the birds and insects that have also made their home here, I think our case will be very strong. There are almost no green spaces in the city and they are needed."

There is that word "green" again. I know that without rain nothing will turn green and even here there hasn't been much rain.

"We do have to be careful though, Palma," Isaac says. "Wabenzi is capable of threatening people with violence if they get in his way. He knows about your work."

Palma laughs.

"What – he'll even threaten visiting scientists like me?"

"Yes," Isaac answers. "He can make it look like an accident or a robbery gone wrong."

Isaac and Palma have their backs to the big gate that they came in through. As Chibwe and I watch from our hideout in the bushes we see three men with sticks come in. They're hunched over so that they can sneak up quietly behind Palma and Isaac. One of the men I recognise. It's Mr Badman from the bar.

My mouth is open to shout a warning but I don't want Mr Badman to see me and Chibwe and maybe to find Masika. I must think. I must remember something. There is the flutter of bird's wings disturbed by the men. A bird flies up into the tree. I'm reminded of a bee-eater and then I see it. I tug at Chibwe's shoulder and point at it.

"Chibwe look! Can you see that bees' nest? Can you hit it with a stone?"

Just over the heads of Mr Badman and the two men is a small swarm of bees clumped together and hanging from the branch of a msasa tree. The sounds of the other insects and birds and the focus of the men on Isaac and Palma means that they don't hear the buzzing bees. Chibwe doesn't wait. In one moment he has a fist-sized rock in his hand and in the next it is whizzing through the air straight towards the bee swarm. The men jump upright in horror at the sound of the stone hurtling through the bee's nest and lift their sticks over their heads. The bees explode into a furious stinging cloud ready to attack anything that moves. Shouting and batting their sticks at the bees, the men are forced to run back out of the gate and away from the secret wilderness. Fortunately for the rest of us, the bee swarm chases after them.

Isaac and Palma keep still and quiet until the angry bees have gone. It's obvious to me that they understand how insects behave. Even so Isaac has managed to carefully use his camera to photograph the men.

"They were going to attack us!" he says angrily. "Did Wabenzi send them?"

"Who threw the stone at the bee's nest?" Palma asks, astonished. She turns in our direction and sees us.

"Who are you?" she asks.

"Who are you?" Chibwe demands right back and he folds his arms and stares at her.

"I'm sorry," she says at once. "I'm Palma and this is Isaac. I think you saved us from being beaten up by those men – thank you – but how did you come here and why did you help us?"

"The birds and bees saved you," I say. "My brother, Chibwe, has a stronger arm for throwing than me so he was better at hitting the bees."

"Chipo comes here to collect healing herbs for my Aunt," Chibwe says. Neither of us want to mention Masika but he's heard the men shouting and so he comes up to us and stands behind Chibwe.

"That was Mr Badman who wanted to beat you both," he says to Isaac. "He works for Mr Wabenzi and so do the other men. They are the ones who kidnap street children."

Isaac and Palma stare at Masika.

"So, you were right, Isaac," Palma says. "This Mr Wabenzi did arrange for us to be attacked!"

"Is there another way out of here?" Isaac asks. "Those men might wait outside for us – or the bees may come back and still be angry."

Chibwe and I show Isaac and Palma the gap between the wall and the fence. As we go, we tell them what we are doing in the secret wilderness.

"It's wonderful that we've met you both!" Palma says. "Perhaps you can all help me? I want to record and photograph all the different plants, birds and insects that live in this place. I don't have long and you can show me all the things you know so I can do it quickly and we can stop the plans to build on this little wilderness – I can pay you for your work."

"I'll arrange for a security guard to watch the gate so those men don't come back and I'll show the photos of them to the police," Isaac says.

Chibwe and I look at each and we smile and laugh.

"This is the best thing that's happened to us for a long time!" Chibwe says and Masika does a dance stamping his feet and waggling his bottom.

CHAPTER TEN
WATER IS LIFE

Chibwe and I really enjoy working with Isaac and Palma at listing and photographing all the plants and creatures in the secret wilderness. I explain to Palma what Ma would have done with the medicinal herbs. Chibwe tells her the names he knows for all the trees and she shows him pictures of them in her books and explains that some of them are related to each other. Because we've spent so long there with Masika we can show Palma where different birds make their nests and where there are the homes of hundreds of different insects. Masika tells them about the night he was visited by a jackal and the morning he woke up to find a flock of guinea fowl running through the grass. He doesn't mention that he managed to trap and eat one, and Chibwe and I keep his secret too.

"You are my research team," Palma says. "I'll pay you for the time you are here. It won't be much but I will add your names to my report. What we are discovering is that this is a new wilderness that has grown up and is rich in many different kinds of life all of which is good for us too."

"You won't believe it," Isaac tells us. "Only fifty years ago all the trees were chopped down on this land and the grass was cut short so that big aeroplanes could land and take off. It's a miracle how nature can regenerate and grow back into beautiful woodland again."

"There are good Spirits here," I say. "Can you all feel them around us?"

Everybody nods. We are all sitting down by the pool of water in the middle of the wilderness watching and making notes about the birds that come down to drink there.

"Ma says that water is life," I say, remembering my mother's wisdom.

"That's so true!" Palma says. "Life began in the oceans of earth billions of years ago and all life depends on it. Even people are made mostly of water."

"The water in this pool is so clear and clean." Chibwe puts his fingers into the pool and we see a frog splash into it at the opposite end. "Why isn't it dirty and muddy like the rain puddles in town?"

"The plants and grasses that grow around it and the insects and small animals that use it help to filter the water and keep it clean. It is a healthy balance," Palma explains. "It's a pool and not a river so we will have to look after it so that it isn't overgrown or damaged."

Isaac smiles. "People who live beside rivers must look after them too. Cutting down trees beside rivers causes floods."

David arrives to see how Masika is doing and to make sure that Chibwe and I are still looking after him. It turns out that he and Isaac are friends.

"Its good to meet you Palma," David says. "The work you're doing is so important. We can all see what a positive effect it's had on Masika. Imagine how it would help all the other orphans too if there was a green park they could visit."

***

Chibwe and I reckon we will soon have enough money to buy our tickets for the minibus journey all the way to the banks of the Great River.

"Will we have to pay someone to take us up the Great River to the Evergreen Forest? Perhaps we won't have enough money for that?" I ask.

"Somebody will be going there anyway and they'll let us go with them," Chibwe says.

"How do you know that?" I ask crossly.

We've begun to argue with each other all the time.

"Are we going to tell Aunt Chimunya that we are going to leave?" I ask.

"We can't tell her," Chibwe says. "She'll stop us going, won't she?"

"Perhaps Cousin Faith will be better and Aunt Chimunya will come with us?"

"Even if Aunt Chimunya can leave Faith she still won't take us with her, will she?" Chibwe replies.

I think that Chibwe is right

"I don't feel it's right to leave without telling Aunt Chimunya, all the same."

It's so complicated that I begin to cry.

"I think I'll have to go by myself," Chibwe says. "Then I'll have enough money to pay a boatman to take me up the river. Besides you are too little and too young! You can stay and help Aunt Chimunya."

"If you dare do that, I'll hate you for ever!" I shout.

CHAPTER ELEVEN
MA RICHWOMAN

I run off and spend that afternoon all by myself with Palma in the little wilderness.

"Is something wrong, Chipo?" she asks. "You seem very unhappy."

At first, I don't want to say anything but Palma just waits quietly for me to speak.

"It's Chibwe," I say at last. "We have to go on a long journey and Chibwe thinks he should go by himself and leave me here in the city with my Aunt Chimunya."

"Perhaps he's trying to be sensible and take care of you?" Palma says. "Do tell me. What journey are you going to make and why?"

"I don't know if you'll believe me," I say, but then I do tell Palma everything.

"You know what, Chipo," Palma tells me. "I think your journey is necessary and getting the help of Makemba is very important for your family and maybe for all of us too. You've shown me that you are as brave as Chibwe and I think nothing is going to stop both of you going to the Evergreen Forest. Give me a little time – maybe I can help you both when I've finished my work here."

Palma digs in her backpack and pulls out two objects.

"Chipo – here's a folding penknife and an aluminium water bottle with a carry-bag to put them in. They'll be useful on your trip. I'll see you tomorrow and we'll talk about what else I can do."

Palma gives me a hug and I thank her for her kindness.

"Go and tell Chibwe," she says, smiling.

Chibwe is as pleased as I am at Palma's gifts.

"It will be much better if we do both travel together," he says. "And we could use the help of someone like Palma."

We both feel so happy that we don't watch out for trouble as carefully as we usually do on our way home. We've walked straight past the bus station and the shops. I wave at William Mukuka as we go by but I'm so sure that everything will be all right from now on that I don't notice the big shiny black Mercedes with the smoked windows parked by the roadside. We carry on walking. I don't even see its doors open until my hair is pulled very hard and I hear Chibwe shout and see him also put his hands up to his head.

Ma Richwoman has come up behind us and has grabbed both Chibwe and me by our hair in her two enormous hands.

"Ah! Got you both!" she shouts. "Wretched brats that you are! Teach you to think you can be smart and escape me! I know where you live anyway but I've got you now! I've got customers waiting for you both!"

Ma Richwoman jerks us both off our feet and starts to drag us back to her car. I can see as I twist my neck that her chauffeur has opened the car boot and is on his way to help her with us. All I can see of Ma Richwoman is the bright neon pink dress around her huge body.

"It's all over for Chibwe and me!" I think and I shut my eyes.

I feel an enormous bump and hear the sounds of slapping and screams.

Ma Richwoman is screeching "Get off me! Get off me!"

Chibwe and I fall on the ground. We are both free.

"Run! Run! Get away as fast as you can!"

It's William. He has seen our danger and he's organised a gang of street kids to come to our rescue. They are running around Ma Richwoman and her chauffeur – they've taken her handbag and her car keys. They're pulling at her skirt. They're kicking her legs. They're throwing rubbish at her and tripping up her chauffeur. William is squirting a plastic bottle of dirty brown liquid in Ma Richwoman's face.

"Run! Run!" It's Chibwe shouting this time. He's taken my hand. We turn around and run as fast as possible to the bus station.

"Just get on the mini-bus!" Chibwe says. "It's this one. We pay when we're on it. It's leaving now!"

And that's exactly what we do. We duck down low and push our way past the knees and legs of the adult passengers as if we know that our parents are just ahead of us. An old woman is struggling to get her basket onto her lap and she leaves the tiniest gap on the seat by the window. Chibwe squeezes himself sideways onto the seat and pulls me onto his knee just as we hear Ticket Boss shout out that the bus is full.

"No more room! Get off the step! We're leaving! Out!"

Ticket Boss waves a fistful of money in one hand and shoves a man out of the door with the other. I'm surprised he doesn't fall out too.

"You were going to leave without me, Chibwe! That's how you know it's this bus, don't you!" I say. I'm shocked that he thought of going without me but also very grateful that he knew which bus it would be.

"Yes!" Chibwe says. "I changed my mind because of Palma. But now I know that it wouldn't be safe to leave you because Ma Richwoman would have caught you and made you a slave again."

"Is she following us?" I ask, jerking my neck in terror as I try to see behind us.

Chibwe shakes his head. "William squirted dirty water in her eyes. I don't think she saw which way we went!"

"Oh!" I say. "Oh! At last we're on our way!"

PART THREE

THE JOURNEY

CHAPTER ONE
MR WABENZI'S ROAD

The minibus spews out a cloud of blue smoke as it coughs and splutters its way from the bus station. It stops, starts, and halts at the red traffic lights. It seems that the lights are broken. The passengers shout at the driver until he edges the minibus forward bit by bit from one gap in the traffic to another space between cars. The city air is a stifling dirty-grey and the hooting is deafening.

"How long will it take to get to the Small Town on the Great River?" I ask Chibwe.

"It's supposed to take all day – about eight hours," Chibwe says. He grins at me. "At this speed I think it'll take us eight weeks."

We both giggle with fear and relief. The old woman we are squashed up against gives us a tolerant smile. We smile back and Chibwe greets her politely calling her Grandmother.

"Good morning, Ma Gogo. I hope that you are well."

"Good morning, children," she answers. "It will take less time than that once we leave the city. This driver is too fast. We call him Mr Speedy."

I'm not sure that I want to be driven by a Mr Speedy who is too fast.

"Is he a safe driver, Ma Gogo?" I ask, but the old woman just smiles.

"Where are you going? Where are your parents?" she asks. Chibwe and I look at each other.

"Our Grandparents live in the Small Town on the Great River." Chibwe says. "Our mother has gone there already to find us a house." I nod my head to show that this is true.

"My name is Mary and my brother here is called Ben, Ma Gogo," I lie.

I don't like telling lies to Ma Gogo, but I'm afraid Mr Wabenzi will find us.

"What about Aunt Chimunya? She'll be worried. What about Masika? What about Palma?" I whisper to Chibwe.

"I don't know what to do. I feel bad about upsetting them too," he whispers back. "We'll write a letter to them when we get to the Small Town."

"Perhaps somebody will phone for us? What about Ma and Pa?"

Chibwe squeezes my hand.

"We're doing this for them!"

At last the minibus leaves the city centre and we find ourselves on a long straight road driving past small houses and small gardens. The minibus goes faster and faster and the houses get smaller and the gardens bigger until we come to big farms and finally to the open countryside where we are among tall trees and green shrubs. That's when the minibus starts to go a little slower and to swerve from side to side along the road. We are flung about with the sharp movements the driver is making and I bang my head on the minibus window.

"What's happening, Ma Gogo?" I ask, holding my bruised ear.

Ma Gogo is using her arm to brace herself against the side of the minibus.

"This road was planned" – bump – "by Mr Wabenzi." – bump – "He did not pay the workers their money" – bump – "so they did not build it well." – bump – "The rain gets under the road surface" – bump- "and it makes big potholes." – bump- bang!

I can see some of the potholes in the road from out of the window. In some places the road is only potholes and then the minibus driver leaves the road and drives alongside it.

Everybody knows about Mr Wabenzi. Mr Wabenzi seems to be everywhere and to be in charge of everyone. I think there are probably lots of Mr Wabenzis and Ma Richwomans. Are there enough good people like Ma and Pa and Palma and Isaac and David to make the world safe? What do the Spirits have to tell me about all of this? Will we ever be able to escape from the Wabenzis in the world? Here we are running away from Kambili and the drought in our Valley but wherever we go, we seem to be in more danger from the Mr Wabenzis.

"Ma Gogo," I ask, looking up at her. "Who is Mr Wabenzi? I've never heard of him. What does he do?"

"Ah Mary child," Ma Gogo answers on a smoother stretch of road. "Mr Wabenzi is very rich. First, he owned some land, then he became the boss of some mines. Next he bought some politicians and made them work for him. Now he thinks that he owns all of us. It's best not to speak of Mr Wabenzi except in whispers. He is very powerful and he has spies everywhere. Even on this minibus."

I can't think of anything to say. There's nowhere to hide on the minibus. Chibwe is silent too. All we can do is settle down and wait till we get to the Small Town.

"Who is most likely to be Mr Wabenzi's spy on this bus?" I wonder. "Does Ma Gogo know?"

In spite of the bumps and the swinging of the minibus, I fall asleep against Ma Gogo's side. It's soft and comfortable, unlike Chibwe's bony knees.

***

Several hours later the minibus arrives at a fuel station and bar in a village. A few people leave the minibus and even more people get on. Some women come by selling bananas and sweets. A young man climbs out of a window and goes to the wash room. When he returns, he has an argument with Ticket Boss who says that he must pay again. The other passengers shout at Ticket Boss that the young man has already paid.

"I suppose Ticket Boss wanted the money for himself," Ma Gogo says.

I notice that Ticket Boss is listening to somebody on his phone. The conversation worries him and he frowns. He starts to check on the people on the minibus. It's too crowded for him to get into the bus so he walks around it and looks in through the windows. I make myself small and try and hide under Ma Gogo's armpit.

"Is this boy with you, Ma Gogo?" Ticket Boss asks her over the top of Chibwe's head.

"Yes," Ma Gogo answers leaning on top of me. "What's it to you, Ticket Boss?"

"I'm looking for two runaway children who are thieves!" he replies.

"Huh! You minibus people are the runaway thieves with your high fares and broken down buses. Leave us good people alone!" Ma Gogo says.

"I'll watch you, Ma Gogo! You get off half-way that means the boy will have to get off there too!"

Then Ticket Boss turns back to his phone.

"There are two kids on the minibus," he says. "but this old woman says they are her relations."

He listens again.

"I can't stop the minibus here. The passengers will be very angry. The driver won't agree in case they damage his minibus."

"Okay!" he says a minute later.

I wonder who he's talking to and I can see that Chibwe is as worried as I am.

Ticket Boss speaks to the driver but the driver shakes his head and the minibus starts off again. Mr Speedy is living up to his name. The bus goes faster and faster. For the first hour nobody complains though Ticket Boss looks rather annoyed. From his seat by the door he keeps looking back down the road to the city as if he expects that someone is following behind. The journey goes on and on, hour after hour. I doze again against the softness of Ma Gogo.

I'm fast asleep when the minibus crashes.

CHAPTER TWO
THE ACCIDENT

I'm dreaming when the minibus crashes.

It's the hottest time of day. It's quiet because most of the other passengers are tired and no one is talking loudly any more. I don't cry out because I don't know what is happening. In my dream I've fallen out of an eagle's nest and it seems to me that my dream carries on and on and I keep on plummeting towards the ground for a long time until I hear Chibwe call out my name. I find myself lying on top of Ma Gogo with Chibwe spread out on top of me. The minibus is on its side. We aren't hurt at all but we've knocked the air out of Ma Gogo's lungs and she's huffing and puffing in fright. Children and babies are crying. Passengers are scrambling out of the doors and windows and shouting at the driver and Ticket Boss.

"Why were you going so fast, Mr Speedy?"

"Give us our money back, Ticket Boss!"

It's confusing and noisy.

The driver hit such a deep pothole that at first it slowed the minibus down, then unbalanced it and tipped it gently over into a sausage tree. One of the tree's giant sausage-like fruits is still swinging loose and banging against the cracked windscreen.

The driver is the only person who has bumped his head enough to make it bleed and though everyone is angry and a few are bruised and frightened, no one seems badly hurt. The passengers start to look for the baggage that's rolled off the roof rack and to collect their possessions together.

Ticket Boss stops arguing about giving the passengers their fares back and he's on his phone again. Something makes me go up close behind him so I can listen to what he's saying. Chibwe has the same idea.

"We've crashed," Ticket Boss says. "We're still a long way from the Small Town. The kids are still here. Are you far behind us? Yes – I know the road is bad! How much longer?"

He is surrounded again by the irate passengers and has to put his phone back in his pocket.

"My luggage is damaged."

"The fruit I was carrying is all spoilt and bruised."

"I want compensation."

"What's going to happen now?"

"How are we going to get to the Small Town today?"

Chibwe and I slide away behind the sausage tree.

"I think Ticket Boss is Mr Wabenzi's spy," Chibwe says.

I nod in agreement. "We need to get away from here somehow."

We look around. The thick woodlands we've travelled through have changed into open grassy plains. There are no villages nearby and the only road we can see is a rough and broken track that tilts away to the north-west over hilly and rocky ground.

"There's nowhere to hide."

"We can't run faster than Ticket Boss."

"Who do you think is following us? Mr Wabenzi or somebody who works for him?"

"We need the wings of birds," I say, but our feet are planted on the roadside.

"Listen! I can hear a car coming!" I say nervously and I tug at Chibwe to make him run. He stands still and concentrates for a moment.

"It's not a Mercedes – I think it's an old four-wheel drive – it's quite slow – and it's already close to us."

We watch fascinated as an old jeep draws up next to the crashed minibus. An old white-haired woman and an old grey-haired man both wearing faded safari clothes and saggy bush hats climb out of it.

"Dear-oh-dear-oh-dear!" says the man. "What-have-we-got-here? Is anybody hurt? Can we help?"

His companion, the old woman, repeats the old man's questions in three different languages and soon everybody on the bus is replying and there are at least four different languages to listen to all at the same time.

Chibwe and I stare at the two old people and their jeep. The old grey-haired man wears spectacles and his pale-brown skin is dotted with big yellow and brown freckles. His white-haired wife has a black skin with big white splotches on her face and arms. The jeep is packed with camping gear, extra fuel cans and cold-boxes of food. I can see books and binoculars like those that Palma and Isaac use.

"I think we can trust them!" I whisper to Chibwe. "They're bird watchers and wilderness people."

While everyone is talking to the old couple, we make our way behind the minibus and around to the back of the jeep.

"Can you give me a lift to the Small Town please?" one of the passengers asks the old couple.

"Please – I need the lift most of all," someone else says.

"No. Sorry. We can't," the old man answers. "We're not going that way at all. We're taking that rough road across the flood plain there." And he points down the track that goes north-west.

The old woman repeats his answer in the three different languages that she knows and after a bit everyone quietens down and puts on expressions that show they are sad and disappointed. While this is going on Chibwe and I climb into the foot-well in the back of the jeep where we cover ourselves with a loose tarpaulin that we find. It's hot and sweaty under it but perhaps no one will look for us here. What are the chances that they'll notice we're missing? What are the chances that Ma Gogo will ask what's happened to us?

"We've got a long way to go tonight, Winnie," the old man says.

"We must get on our way, Wally," the old woman replies.

They come back to the jeep and it shifts under their weight as they climb in and sit down. The engine starts and the jeep moves off. We feel it cross the road, go down into the ditch, up the other side until it starts to bump off along the track to the north-west. My nose and one eye are peeking out from under the tarpaulin. I can see Ma Gogo. She is looking at the jeep as it leaves and she gives a tiny nod and a little secret wave with her hand in our direction.

"Where are those kids?" Ticket Boss is saying to her.

"It's not your business, Ticket Boss," Ma Gogo answers

pointing away from the jeep. "They've gone to make a pee in the bushes. You just have to wait for them to come back."

CHAPTER THREE
WALLY AND WINNIE

The floor of the jeep on which Chibwe and I are lying is hard and uncomfortable. Dust rises up from under the jeep's wheels and through the open sides. It chokes us and the heat and smell of the old vehicle made us feel sick, but the old man drives his vehicle with great care over the rocks and bumps so that we lurch about slowly and steadily and aren't flung around as we were in the minibus. As the jeep goes down an incline, we roll forwards, and when it goes up a steep slope we roll backwards. All we can hear is the noise of the engine and its transmission. Before we've gone very far over the rough track, the jeep comes to a standstill and its engine is turned off. In the sudden quiet we can hear in the distance behind us the faint sounds of shouting people and a car's hooter parping and parping endlessly.

"What's going on back there Winnie?" the old man says.

"Hand me the binoculars, Wally, and I'll have a look," she answers.

There's a moment of silence, then Winnie speaks again.

"A black Mercedes has arrived and is parked by the minibus. Somebody is waving in our direction and someone else is hooting. Do you think they want us to go back for some reason?"

"We're already too far away," Wally says. "What could they possibly want us for?"

"Oh, my goodness!" Winnie says. "Now there's a fight! The passengers are banging on the roof of the Mercedes and shouting – you can just hear them. Do we need to go and help?"

"If minibus passengers are angry with the driver of a Mercedes, I would guess they've got good reasons," Wally suggests.

The possibility that the old man and woman might go back to the minibus and the Mercedes is too much for me and Chibwe. We push the tarpaulin off our dusty heads and try to speak. All I can do is cough and try to breathe air, not dust.

"No! Please don't go back!" Chibwe begs. "The man in the Mercedes wants to make us prisoners and maybe kill us. Please – don't go back! Please save us!"

Chibwe too, begins to cough. We both have tears running down our cheeks.

The old man leaps out of the jeep. The splotches of brown on his face look darker because he has become pale with fright. He bangs his hand against his chest. His wife gives a little start then shakes her head quickly.

"Heavens Wally! Don't panic! It's just two children in need of help."

She turns to us.

"Stop crying and tell us what you're doing here. Where are your parents?"

"Please, drive us away from here!" Chibwe begs again.

"Will they follow us? Are they following?" I cry and cough.

"Wally, lets go!" Winnie says. "Cross that rocky river bed down there where we'll leave no tracks and then stop among those trees where we can talk without being seen.

"No Mercedes is going to come down this road," she says to Chibwe and me. "No one will be able to follow our tracks either on this stony ground. Get out from under the tarpaulin both of you and sit on the seat so you can breathe."

***

I'm still crying quietly when we finally stop in a small grove of trees after another half hour's driving. Chibwe has curled himself over so his head is on his knees and his arms are over his head.

"These kids are extremely afraid," Wally observes.

"They've survived a car crash," Winnie says. "Something else is wrong though – they do seem traumatised."

She spreads a rug on the ground and makes us sit down on it while she wipes our faces with a damp rag and looks us over to see if we are hurt.

"Just bruised, I think, but also needing food and drink."

Winnie gives us tin mugs of cool water from a big container and makes us eat bread thickly covered with guava jam and peanut butter.

"When you're both feeling better you can tell us what's going on," Wally says.

I try to explain but thinking about all that's happened makes me cry again so Chibwe takes over and tells them about Mr Wabenzi and how we had to run away from Ma Richwoman.

"That's an amazing story," Wally says. "But how did you meet Mr Wabenzi? We know all about how bad and dangerous he is."

"Begin at the beginning," Winnie says, and that's when I explain about our search for Makemba and the source of the Great River.

Winnie sighs and turns to Wally. Wally shakes his head and looks back at Winnie.

"We'll take you as far as we can," he says. "We aren't going all the way to the Great River. At this time of year, rains from the Faraway North begin to fill up the Great River until all the floodplain around it is covered with water. It's not possible to drive our jeep across it."

"Every person who cares about birds and insects and plants and trees knows that your journey is necessary to end the drought," Winnie tells us. "We can't go instead of you but we will help as much as we can."

I jump up, run to Winnie and throw my arms around her middle.

"Whoa! Whoa!" says Wally, looking nervous and pleased. He reaches out to shake my hand then he shakes Chibwe's. Winnie hugs Chibwe and Chibwe and I hug each other. We are so glad to be with them both and to feel safe once again.

I don't want to think what we may have to do next. I don't want to think about what may be happening to Ma and to Pa back in the Valley. As long as we are driving as far away from Mr Wabenzi as possible, I feel safer. All I want is to carry on riding in the jeep with Winnie and Wally while I eat guava jelly and peanut butter sandwiches.

CHAPTER FOUR
THE FOREVER GRASSLANDS

The grasslands are never-ending. My eyes can't tell how far they stretch before the whole world appears to curve away from me. The wind strokes the grasses, soothing them and stirring them into waves and patterns so they are forever singing and sighing to themselves while the sunlight flickers and dances on their leaves and seed heads. I know that this is another place that is full of good Spirits.

"It's like being on the ocean," Wally says, his eyes narrowing against the sun. "We can see far away to what sailors call the offing – that's the edge of the world that's too distant for us to see anything coming."

"It's a dreaming world," Winnie says. "Whenever we're here I want to stay forever."

"I feel like that too," I say to Chibwe. "I feel that nothing else matters."

"The movement of the grasses is hypnotising," Chibwe agrees and I know the Spirits are talking to him too and to Wally and Winnie.

The jeep is parked on the edge of huge plains of grass and we've been sitting here for hours watching different antelope grazing in front of us.

"There are puku, lechwe, and buffalo down there. What else can you see?" says Wally, handing his binoculars to Chibwe.

"There are some hippo feeding near that lagoon," Chibwe

says, pointing. "They must feel safe here even though it's midday."

Wally and Winnie spend all day watching wild animals. Chibwe and I sit down beside them and they tell us all about the different creatures we can see. Winnie loves insects. She shows me her butterfly net.

"This is how you catch butterflies without hurting them," she says. "Once you have caught them in the net, hold it up over them so they are safe but not hurt. You can photograph and identify what kind of butterfly you've caught before letting them go free."

Wally and Winnie know the Latin names of every bird they see while Chibwe and I know the names we call them at home.

"Latin names are understood around the world and written in books," Wally says.

"Our names tell us what the birds are like and how they behave," Chibwe tells him.

"Some birds live here all the year but there are others who fly from across the world to visit the Great River when it floods," Winnie says.

Chibwe and I keep on asking questions but even Winnie and Wally don't know all the answers to everything. Winnie asks us about our life on the farm and the kinds of animals that live in our Valley.

"The Valley has a different climate and environment," she says. "There are giraffe in your Valley and there are none here, so you know things that I don't."

"Knowing how to ask questions is more useful than knowing

the answers," Wally says. "That's how we find out how our world works."

"There may only be one way to beat the Drought Witch," Winnie tells us. "If you look after all the wild creatures, insects and birds too, if you protect the trees and grasses, you can stop the Drought Witch taking over your land."

"Everything has to work together. Everything is connected and even if things change everything has to find a balance," Wally explains.

"That's what Palma told us about the trees and birds in the Secret Wilderness in the Big City," I say.

Then I remember Mr Wabenzi.

"Mr Wabenzi and his friend, Mr Willie Waffell are going to start mining in the Valley. Won't that be very bad?"

Winnie and Wally both nod their heads in time with each other.

"That will be very bad!" says Winnie.

"Nobody can stop him!" says Wally.

We are all silent. I've asked a question and nobody has any answers.

Chibwe scowls and Winnie pats his shoulder. I notice the blotches of white on the skin of her hands.

"Why is your skin like that?" I ask. Chibwe's head jerks towards me. He waggles one finger in front of his mouth. He thinks I shouldn't ask that question.

"It's a condition called Vitiligo." Winnie says. "Some parts of my skin have no pigment, so they have no colour."

"It makes you look like one of those beautiful wild dogs," I say. "They have dark and light patches too."

Wally and Winnie laugh.

"What kind of animal do I look like Chipo?" Wally asks.

"Your spots are more like a baby hyena or a jackal," I answer, and this time everybody laughs.

"What about us?" Chibwe asks. "What animals are we like?"

"You two are very handsome animals of a beautiful colour," Wally says.

"You two are also very dirty animals!" Winnie says. "Next time we get to a river you'll have to have a proper wash with soap!"

Chibwe and I enjoy travelling with Wally and Winnie because our life is easy, we have tasty food to eat and full stomachs. Winnie has tins of home-made biscuits and cakes for tea. Wally cooks sausages and lamb chops on the fire for supper and we eat potatoes, tomatoes, bananas and oranges. At night Winnie makes us a comfortable bed in the jeep under a mosquito net while Wally puts up a tent for the two of them. Wally makes little grunting sounds like a small hippo when he sleeps while Winnie whistles and hoots like an owl, but that doesn't stop me and Chibwe from enjoying a deep restful sleep.

CHAPTER FIVE
THE MUDDY PLAIN

Several days later we stop on a rocky ridge of land in the early morning and we all climb out of the jeep to look around us. In the far distance where the sun sets, I can see the shiny gleam of a large river or lake and a curl of white smoke rising straight up into the blue sky.

"This is as far as we can drive," Wally says. "From here the ground is soft and muddy and the jeep will sink into it up to its axles and get stuck."

"That smoke comes from a fishing village on the Great River," Winnie says. "It's the home of Chief Ikabonga. That is where you need to go. Chief Ikabonga will tell you how to get to the Evergreen Forest."

"It'll take you all day to walk there," Wally says. "You mustn't stop walking and you must keep your eyes on that smoke otherwise you'll be lost and go around in circles."

Chibwe and I give each other anxious looks.

"How does the ground get so muddy and wet when there has been no rain?" Chibwe asks. "Where does the water come from?"

"The water comes from heavy rains that fall in the Faraway North, that's another country," Wally tells us. "It soaks into the ground there and then gradually arrives here by seeping into small streams and underground rivers."

"It's like magic isn't it?" Winnie says. "There are many other places in the world where this happens. That's how some rivers can be full in the dry season with water from faraway."

I haven't worried about Ma and Pa and the Valley and I haven't thought about our journey to find Makemba for a while. Ever since we met Wally and Winnie I've been living in a happy dream. That has to change now that we are setting off alone again. I hope that Ma and Pa are not feeling as lonely as Chibwe and I are.

"Please Winnie," I ask. "When you get back to the Big City tell Aunt Chimunya what happened and say she mustn't worry about us."

"Please, can you post a letter to Ma and Pa from us too?" Chibwe asks.

"Of course!" Winnie says. "Wally and I will certainly do that for you!"

***

Now Chibwe and I must set off alone again without knowing what will happen next. I tuck my head under Winnie's patterned arm to hide my tears.

Winnie rubs my head.

"Let's get you what you need for your walk," she says. "Food and water – you have a water bottle and a penknife."

"I know you'll look after each other," Wally says to Chibwe. "We need you to fight the Drought Witch and win."

He gives Chibwe an encouraging slap on his back that almost knocks him over. It only takes a few moments for Winnie to give us some food and water. I think she must have packed it ready for us last night.

"I've put a packet of fish-hooks for you to give Chief Ikabonga when you get there," Winnie says. "It's always best to not go empty-handed to visit someone like Chief Ikabonga. He will be pleased with such a useful gift."

Winnie hugs us and Wally shakes our hands. We say goodbye and thank them both for rescuing us.

"We'll miss you both," we say.

We set off walking down from the ridge and onto a muddy track that seems to go in the direction of the fishing village. It is already hot. We don't look back at first. From the lower muddy track, we can't see the shining water, just the thin feather of white smoke dissolving into the sky.

***

When we are forced to stop to scrape the clods of mud from our trainers we turn around and look back towards Winnie and Wally's jeep. Chibwe screws up his eyes.

"Can you see them?" he asks. "Is that their jeep? It looks like a big brown rock to me."

"I don't know," I answer. "It's the same colour as the jeep but I can't see any people."

"Are those animals running away from it?" Chibwe asks. "Where are Wally and Winnie?"

"Were they real or a dream?" I wonder, but the bag of food and water I'm carrying feels real and heavy.

"Let's get on," Chibwe says. "I'll carry the bag for a while."

We set off again and the sun that was burning our left shoulder moves over onto our heads and feels as hot as fire. We take off our trainers and walk barefoot over the soggy earth. It's easier to get the caked mud off our bare feet than off our shoes. When the sun is right above us, we stop for water and food. The smoke is beginning to fade away when we start walking again.

"As long as the sun isn't shining into our eyes in the next few hours, we'll be going in the right direction," Chibwe says.

I walk behind him hoping he is right. We go on and on and on. We are both tired and there is no more smoke to see.

"Animals made this path. It keeps turning," I say.

"True," Chibwe answers. "But these animals are going towards the water and they never go in a straight line. We will get to the river."

I think I see smoke again but it's behaving strangely. It doesn't go straight up – it curves up and then loops back.

"Chibwe look!" I shout. "Look there are flocks of birds over there – they must be flying over the river – they're birds that live near water!"

We turn to each other smiling and laughing. I even jump up and down on my muddy feet. We carry on walking with more hope. Once again, we see the smoke from a fire starting to rise upwards and spiral in a light afternoon breeze. We are much closer to the river and the day is beginning to cool a little too. Soon we hear sounds of voices from Chief Ikabonga's village. I wonder what he is like and who else lives there. My heartbeats quicken, and my feet move faster.

Chibwe and I come to a sudden stop. I clutch at Chibwe's arm. There are some dogs on the path in front of us barking and snarling with their teeth bared ready to attack us.

"Will they bite us?" I start to say but before I finish speaking, we are surrounded by more than twenty children laughing and shouting.

"Who are you?"

"Where have you come from?"

"Why are you here?"

"What do you want?"

They chase the dogs away and take us into the middle of the village where their five mothers are tending the fire and preparing food for supper.

"Sit down here and wait," one of the mothers says.

"Go and fetch Chief Ikabonga," another mother says to one of the bigger children.

We wait and wait. I'm beginning to yawn and fall asleep on Chibwe's shoulder when a tall broad-shouldered man strides into the circle around the fire. He wears a red cap with four tall black feathers on it, a white tee-shirt with an elephant printed onto it, and he has a black cloth skirt that's wrapped around his shorts.

"Greetings!" he says. "I am told that you two children have walked across the muddy plain all by yourselves to come to my village. You must have very good reasons to come such a long way. First you must eat and drink. Afterwards you must tell why you have come to see me, the Chief Ikabonga of the Fishing Village – the most important chief on the Great River."

"Greetings, Chief Ikabonga," Chibwe says. "Here is a present for you of fish hooks."

"Thank you!" says Chief Ikabonga. "This is a good present for an important Chief!"

CHAPTER SIX
THE FISHING VILLAGE

Chief Ikabonga's village is on a high bank above the wide river. The Great River below it is as grey and smooth as the evening sky and gleams with the pearly light of an early moon. Many fish leap up to catch dancing insects and, as they dive back, they make circles of ripples. Spoonbills dip into the water by the shore and skimmers scoop and dip on the surface of the water. Everywhere birds are flying home to their evening roost.

The five wives of Chief Ikabonga are already busy preparing delicious bottle-nosed fish for the village meal but Chief Ikabonga claps his hands and tells them to carry on doing exactly what they were already doing.

"You see how obedient my five wives are!" he says. "You see how respectful they are and how many children they have given me. You see what a strong man I am. Those are my dug-out canoes – my many mokoro on the river. Those are my brothers in the next village who catch the fish we eat. You see how important I am."

Chibwe and I try to show that we are impressed. The youngest three wives of the Chief giggle behind their hands and the First Wife bangs her wooden spoon several times on the saucepan she's using and looks annoyed. Chibwe and I wonder whether she is cross with the Junior Wives or with the Chief. The Chief's fourteen daughters, including the two-year old baby girl, stand around waiting to help their mothers serve supper. The Chief's eleven sons sit around waiting to be given their food while the Chief's five dogs are waiting at a distance is the hope of leftover scraps. At last the food is cooked and ready. The smell of the fish and the emptiness in my belly make me lick my lips and swallow. Chief Ikabonga claps his hands again and he and his two brothers are given plates of food.

"Chibwe, you are the hero who has walked across the Muddy Plains to my village, though you are young, come and eat with me and my brothers," he says.

Chibwe folds his arms across his chest and stands up straight.

"Chipo, my sister, is my friend and my hero," he says in a clear loud voice. "Chipo, my sister, has also walked across the Muddy Plains with me. She too, must be given food to eat and she must sit with me to eat it."

Everyone is silent. Everyone's mouth is open. Even those who have a mouthful of food stop eating. I don't breathe. Everyone is looking at Chief Ikabonga. Chief Ikabonga stands up and his chest swells. I think he may explode. Instead he throws back his head and laughs and laughs. One by one his brothers, his wives, and his children join in until everyone but Chibwe and me is laughing and even the dogs begin to bark and howl.

"Chipo," Chief Ikabonga says to me, "you, too, are a hero! Come and sit with Chibwe and me and my brothers and eat."

I go to sit with my brother, Chibwe, and the men and the Youngest Wife, still giggling, brings me my dish of fish and maize meal.

"Thank you," I say.

She looks young enough to be at school so I smile at her and she smiles back. I miss going to school. There is so much I want to know and so much more to understand after all that has happened to me and Chibwe. As I am sitting with the men, Chief Ikabonga gives me some home-made maize beer. I know I must not refuse to drink it. My tummy is full, I am so tired. I don't remember falling asleep.

***

I wake in the morning in the women's hut. The hut is made of beautifully patterned grass mats finely woven from the river reeds. Tiny warm spots of sun shine through the textured mats and dance on my face. I wonder where Chibwe has slept and when we will be able to ask Chief Ikabonga to help us find our way to the Evergreen Forest.

Outside the children are bathing in the river while the women do the laundry, wash the pots and pans, and sweep and tidy the yard. The men are mending their fishing nets and their fish traps and cleaning out the dugout canoes. Chibwe is helping them and I can see he is enjoying himself. I walk over to see him and to greet the Chief and his brothers.

"Good morning Chipo, our hero!" Chief Ikabonga says with his huge grin. "How are you this morning? You are just the person I want to see. I have questions for you. Come, sit down here so we can have an indaba – so we can discuss this business. My brothers need your advice."

I can see that Chibwe looks rather alarmed at the idea that I am going to answer the Chief's questions. It was Chibwe who confronted him on my behalf last night, but we do need the Chief's help so it's down to me not to offend him today.

We make ourselves comfortable on the river bank and I turn to Chief Ikabonga and wait. His expression changes and becomes less friendly.

"You are soon going to be old enough to marry, Chipo," he says. "What do you think of that? Will you let your father choose a husband for you?"

Chibwe is sitting beside the Chief. I can see that he's even more worried than I am by this question.

"It's against the law of our land for a girl to marry before she is eighteen years old," I answer. "First of all, a girl must go to school and get an education and that's what I will do."

One of the Chief's brothers nods his head in agreement with me.

"That is so," he says. "Girls should be educated."

The Chief looks furious. He narrows his eyes and considers me with a stern glare. His voice thunders out.

"It's our tradition, Chipo! We must not go against our tradition must we, Chipo? This is what the Spirits of our Ancestors tell us to do isn't it? Tell me – do you believe in the Spirits – do you honour the Spirits – do you obey your father? Why are you and Chibwe making this journey alone?"

There are so many questions. I need to think hard and answer wisely but what must I say that will also be true?

"Tradition is important. You're right," I say. "We make our traditions every day but we make our traditions to fit the present time, don't we?"

I hope that I sound polite and modest.

"I think that's what the Ancestors have always done and isn't that what the Spirits of the Ancestors are telling us to do today?" I carry on.

I can hear both the Chief's brothers murmuring together.

"My daughter tells me that she wants to stay at school until she is old enough to find a job," one of them says and the second brother agrees.

"My wife is a school teacher and she says my daughter must go to school too," he says.

"We have different traditions and laws nowadays," he adds.

"Do you believe in the Spirits, Chipo?" Chief Ikabonga asks me. He sounds a little less angry.

Chibwe interrupts.

"Chipo is close to the Spirits, Chief Ikabonga," he says. "They talk to her and help us both on our journey."

"You also believe in the Spirits, Chibwe," I say, smiling at him.

"The world keeps on changing all the time, Chief Ikabonga, doesn't it?" I suggest.

I hope he is going to agree with us, so I carry on speaking.

"Every day there are more new ideas and more problems to find answers for, aren't there? Nowadays we have cars and motor boats and aeroplanes and schools and universities and so our traditions have to be different and also the same as always."

"How does that work, Chipo?" Chief Ikabonga says. "How is that possible?"

"We must keep the best of our traditions but we must be modern people too." Chibwe answers for me and I just nod my head until it feels as if it's coming loose.

"How can I pay for all my sons and daughters to go to school, Chipo?" Chief Ikabonga asks me.

"Perhaps the oldest children can be the teachers of the youngest children when they've finished school?" I say with a smile.

"Ha!" the Chief replies. "That's a good idea!"

The first brother whose wife is a teacher seems dissatisfied with this idea.

"My wife needs to have pupils who pay her for teaching," he says.

"The Spirits don't have answers for everything," the second brother says. "The Spirits don't understand money."

"Ha!" Chief Ikabonga says. "The Spirits don't understand modern times either! We will have to think about all of this and talk again another time."

Chibwe and I look at each other and then at the ground. We have said enough. At least we hope so.

CHAPTER SEVEN
MAMA WATI

Chibwe and I sit on the banks of the Great River to talk about what we must do next.

"Will Chief Ikabonga help us?" I ask Chibwe.

"I don't know," Chibwe answers. "If he won't I don't know who can. So far, every time something really bad has happened then something good has happened that helped us escape. Maybe we've just run out of luck."

"If we do find Makemba in the Evergreen Forest I don't think we can go back the way we came without getting caught by Mr Wabenzi," I say. "Is there another way home?"

"I don't know," Chibwe answers again.

I don't ask the next question I want to ask about Ma and Pa because Chibwe will have to answer in the same way.

"I don't know if I do believe in the Spirits any more," I say, sinking into misery. "I think the Spirits are tired of us. We aren't the only people who need help, are we? I'm tired too. It's too difficult for us."

Chibwe gives me a sad look. We both are quiet. There's nothing more to say. The Great River flows on past us flickering and swirling in the sun. It tugs at the grasses growing along its shores and they bob down then spring back. We watch a black and white kingfisher hover over the surface, then dive, then hover again and dive until at last it catches a fish. It perches on a branch for a moment in a shower of sparkling water drops before flying off to feed its babies. Butterflies dance, dragonflies zoom, beetles buzz and lizards scurry on busy with their own lives. My thoughts are with Ma and Pa and that reminds me of my Grandmother with her belief in tradition and the Spirits and the Ancestors. I remember that she warned us about dangerous witches riding in whirlwinds. She also told us about the Spirits who live in rivers and swim all the way to the sea and back again.

"Water Spirits need to be respected and rivers need to be cared for by people," she said to us long ago. Sitting by the Great River makes me feel sure that Grandmother is thinking of us.

"The Spirits are here aren't they Chibwe?" I say.

"Yes, they are," Chibwe replies. "Perhaps the Spirits don't need us as much as we need them."

After I've been watching the river for a while, I begin to feel calm and happy again. Chibwe is cheerful once more too. At that moment, I see a smooth black shape rise sideways out of the water. It twists over like a giant fish but, unlike a fish, I see that this shape has a head and neck and looks like a woman. Whatever she is, she looks at me curiously from under a matted mop of reddish curling hair. She is the strangest of water creatures with a human face and round green eyes with heavy lids. Behind each ear I see that she has the gills of a fish. Her dark-skinned, woman-shaped body ends in two writhing fish tails.

"Chibwe, look!" I say, pointing to her. "It's the Water Spirit, the River Mermaid – it's Mama Wati"

As soon as Chibwe sees her, Mama Wati beckons to us, somersaults over, flips her tails and swims back up the Great River towards the Evergreen Forest.

"We've got to find the source of the Great River. That's what she's telling us," Chibwe says. "We have to find where it begins because Makemba will be there. That's all we have to do!"

We both laugh again.

"You make it sound so easy," I say. "Let's go and ask Chief Ikabonga if he can help us."

We get up and go off hand in hand to look for Chief Ikabonga.

We find him still talking to his brothers by their dugout canoes, but they're talking about fishing and the rising water and where they will go tomorrow.

"We've come to ask for your advice and help, Chief Ikabonga," Chibwe says. "We need to set off to the Evergreen Forest to look for the source of the Great River. Please can you tell us if it's possible to go there by boat?"

CHAPTER EIGHT
IMBOLONDO, THE BLACK BULL

"It's not possible for me to take you," Chief Ikabonga explains to us. "I have to be here for the King's Ceremony when the waters rise in a few weeks and so do my brothers. In any case when the land is completely submerged as it will be soon, it is not possible to find a way across it by dugout canoe. There are too many places where even the most experienced fisherman would get lost or be stranded because the river changes its course from moment to moment. I do however, have another idea about how to help you. Come with me now and I'll take you to Imbolondo, my famous black bull."

Chief Ikabonga sets off at a fast pace with Chibwe and I running behind him. He takes us away from the river towards his herd of wide-horned cattle on the grasslands behind his village

"I've never seen such enormous cattle!" Chibwe says in astonishment. "Their horns are huge. They stretch far wider than I can reach with my arms."

The Chief stops and calls out.

"Imbolondo! Imbolondo! Come to me! I have need of you!"

He turns to us.

"This too is our tradition, children. Imbolondo, the black bull of my tribe, has magic powers."

In answer to the Chief's call, the biggest and the blackest bull with the widest horns of all the herd comes towards us.

The ground shakes under his hooves as he moves. He stops right in front of Chief Ikabonga who speaks to him in his deep voice.

"Greetings Imbolondo, the greatest bull of all my herd. I have an important task for you to do. You are needed to carry these two children in safety across the Wide Savannah all the way to the Evergreen Forest."

Imbolondo lowers his head and blows into the Chief's hands. He raises his giant head and bellows loudly. I hear him speak and to my surprise I understand what he's saying even though his voice is so deep and low that only Chibwe and I are close enough to hear it.

"Greetings Chief Ikabonga," Imbolondo says. "I will do as you ask. The Spirits have spoken to me about these two children and I know that their journey is important. Tell them to be ready when the sun rises tomorrow morning and I will carry them safely to the Evergreen Forest as you ask."

***

As the sun rises Chibwe and I make our way from the village to meet Imbolondo. We have with us a large bundle of sun-dried fish and roasted corn cobs prepared by Ikabonga's Five Wives and some sun hats that they have woven for us to wear on our journey. I feel very tiny and feeble standing next to the huge black bull. Chief Ikabonga is standing by the great beast with a handful of green leaves from his Five Wives' gardens for Imbolondo to chew. He looks proud of Imbolondo but also serious. I hope he isn't afraid of what may happen to the three of us.

"Imbolondo is so big. Do you think we will be safe with him?" I whisper to Chibwe. "Is he really a magic beast? Will he listen to us?"

Chibwe is chewing his bottom lip and frowning. He shakes his head.

"I don't know, Chipo," he answers. "We may have to listen to Imbolondo. So far, we have relied on humans to help us. Some have been good people and some have been evil and some have been a mixture of good and bad. It seems to me that the drought and the Drought Witch are not only starving humans but also hurting animals and plants as well. Perhaps we aren't only making this journey to find Makemba for Ma and Pa but for everything that's living as well? In that case maybe it's time to ask for the help of animals too?"

"That's what Malasha said didn't he? – 'Remember the birds! Remember the insects!' – and they did help us, didn't they? Maybe Malasha meant that we should try to help every kind of creature that we can?" I say.

I try to see Imbolondo through the eyes of Malasha or my Grandmother, but I don't think I can manage it.

"My brothers have made a halter for Imbolondo's neck so that you have something to hold onto when you ride. They have also made bags from fishing nets to hold both your food and a bundle of green fodder for Imbolondo to eat," Chief Ikabonga tells us.

Imbolondo snorts, shakes his head from side to side, and rakes the ground with a front hoof. He speaks in his deep low voice that only we can hear.

"Greetings, children! Are you ready for your journey with me? Say goodbye to Chief Ikabonga. It is time to leave!"

We thank Chief Ikabonga, his Five Wives, his twenty-five children and his brothers for their kind hospitality. The Chief shows me how to climb onto Chibwe's shoulders and from there onto Imbolondo's back so that afterwards I can help Chibwe pull himself up as well.

Imbolondo stamps his hooves and kicks out with his back legs.

"So that I see if you are both comfortable," he says. I wonder if black bulls have a sense of humour. Was it amusing for him when I screamed out in fright?

Imbolondo moves off slowly at first. I feel the powerful muscles of his back and the swaying of his body then we are off at a gallop and I'm holding on tight.

"G-goo-ood-ood-b-by-byee-ee – eyow!" we call out as we bounce away.

CHAPTER NINE
THE FREE ANIMALS

Imbolondo did not run fast for long.

"It's not in my nature," he says. "I can but I won't."

Imbolondo stops often to graze.

"I eat slowly," he says. "I digest my food slowly. I need to eat a lot of grass to satisfy my needs. I have many stomachs to do that work and I chew my food twice."

"How long will it take us to reach the Evergreen Forest?" Chibwe asks him.

"It will take as long as it takes," Imbolondo answers.

Chibwe and I look at each other. We make faces and frown at each other. We both know that it would be rude to discuss Imbolondo when we're riding on his back. He understands what we say and it might not be safe to make him cross. I wish I had thought of this before we decided to accept help from him.

"What do you think we should do? Can we make him go faster if we need to?" I don't say the words aloud of course. I try to make my meaning clear by exaggerating the movement of my lips. Chibwe tightens his lips and looks away across the savannah. I hate it when I can't speak. I hate it when I'm ignored.

Imbolondo snorts. I know he's laughing at us. I want to kick him with my heels but he might not feel my kicks or he might just tip me off his back and leave me on the ground. We are already a long way from the Great River.

"Be patient, children," Imbolondo tells us. "You have left

the Valley and your farm. You have left the Big City and your family. You have left the Fishing Village and the Chief. They are all behind you. Now you are in the world of Free Animals. Free Animals do not listen to people. Free Animals do not know time – only day and night, rain and dry, cold and hot and the changing seasons. Free Animals do not obey rules – only what is required by their nature. Children, it is time for each of you to discover what your nature is."

That is such a big thought for me that I can't think of an answer so I decide to keep quiet.

Imbolondo snorts again.

"That is such a big thought for you," he says. "You can't think how to answer it so you will keep quiet." He adds. "Quietness will be your teacher."

Chibwe looks round at me in surprise and he nods. That's when I realise that all three of us have understood each other, Imbolondo, Chibwe and me.

In the world of Free Animals, quietness will be our teacher.

"Listen well. Look widely. Think high, low, near and far. Be a butterfly and a stone," Imbolondo says.

Chibwe and I decide that we will follow his advice. While we were walking alone across the flood plain to the Fishing Village, we didn't see many wild animals. There were some lechwe, a particular species of antelope whose hooves are flattened and specially adapted for walking on soft muddy earth or through shallow water, but on the whole most animals ran away from us even though we're only children. Today Imbolondo is taking us in a different direction, northwards away from the Fishing Village and the Great River onto higher and dryer ground. Close by the village, we passed one or two people who had been to collect firewood in the miombo woodlands but soon we find ourselves in a wilderness without paths or roads where all kinds of animals roam in freedom and none of them run away from us. All these animals are grass-eaters or herbivores, ruminants with many stomachs like Imbolondo. They seem to accept Imbolondo as one of them and not mind that there are two children on his back. We go close up to wildebeest and zebra and even to buffalo. I begin to wonder if we will be safe from lion and cheetah. The thought enters my head and I try to squash it so Imbolondo can't read it.

"Can Imbolondo run fast enough to escape from an attack by a pride of lion?"

I can tell Chibwe is thinking the same thought. He is sitting up very straight and watching the undergrowth around us very carefully.

I suppose it's sensible to concentrate my thoughts on understanding what is happening around me and not on being afraid so I ask him a question in my head.

"Imbolondo, if most animals are grass eaters like you, why does nature also have meat-eaters like lions and wild dogs that hunt them down?"

"If all the animals like me were never hunted by lions and cheetahs and leopards, then there would be so many of us that we would eat up all the grass and die of starvation," Imbolondo answers my thoughts. "In the land of Free Animals, we all obey the rules of our individual natures and that helps to balance all our different needs."

"Does everything stay the same and keep in balance always?" Chibwe asks.

"We have seasons, we have droughts, we have floods and fires. We have plagues and deaths and tragedies," Imbolondo answers. "Nature survives by adapting to change and making a new balance. Even trees learn, change and adapt. We all need each other. The balance of nature is disturbed and upset by people who have no common sense and who have lost touch with their spirits."

"Does that mean that the Free Animals are all friends together?" I ask.

Imbolondo snorts air out of his nostrils and shakes and shivers the skin of his shoulders.

"It's in our nature to respect each other's difference," he says. "It's the nature of meat-eaters to smell different to grass-eaters. It's the nature of grass-eaters to run away from meat-eaters. It's your nature to be omnivores like dogs and pigs."

Chibwe and I both sniff the air to see what Free Animals are nearby. The high savannah air smells clean and dry but we also smell grass and dust and the dung of different grass-eaters. I can smell buffalo dung and I can smell Imbolondo's dung too. It's a good smell, It's the smell of grass and earth and nature.

"It's the nature of the big cats to hide their dung," Imbolondo explains. "So that the smell of their dung does not frighten away the grass-eaters."

"How will we know if there are lions coming to attack us?" Chibwe asks.

"Keep watching," Imbolondo says. "It's in the nature of those meat-eaters that want to kill us to come towards the blowing wind so that the smell of them can't reach us."

Chibwe and I nod.

"Pa taught us about that when we were walking in the Wilderness at home," Chibwe says.

Imbolondo gives his head a big shake and his horns swing dangerously close to us.

"It is in the nature of people to hunt and to eat meat too," he says. "There are people who come here to kill us for food. There are those who kill elephants, lions and leopards for fun."

Chibwe and I have nothing to say. Some things are too complicated to understand at all. Some things are sad.

We are moving along easily in a big herd of striped zebra and shaggy wildebeest together with their foals and calves. Imbolondo keeps stopping to graze while Chibwe and I chew on a mealie cob each. There are white egrets walking under the feet of the animals and a couple of red-billed oxpeckers have joined us on Imbolondo's back.

"Move your knee over," one of the birds says to me. "There's a nice fat tick right there on the bull's back that I want to eat." I tuck my leg up out of the way so it can reach the tick.

"Have you got any ticks that you want to be rid of? I'll eat them up if you like?" The other oxpecker says to Chibwe.

"Of course, I haven't!" Chibwe answers, but I start to scratch my legs just in case a tick has crawled onto me.

"It's the nature of oxpeckers to feast on the ticks that feed on us," Imbolondo says. "It's the nature of egrets to hunt for insects in the earth that the grass-eaters disturb by their grazing. It's the nature of the world for all creatures to depend on each other. It's the nature of the world for creatures to work together and survive or to be at war and die together."

"Chuurh! Churrh! Imbolondo-churrh! Imbolondo-churrh! Wise Bull! Brilliant Beast! Philosopher-churrh!" The oxpeckers shrill and flap and jump their way round to Imbolondo's hindquarters.

"It's the nature of oxpeckers to see the dangers that grass-eaters and children don't see!" says Imbolondo.

"Churrh! Churrh!" call the oxpeckers "Lion attacking! Lion attacking!"

"It's time to run! Hold on children!" bellows Imbolondo.

The oxpeckers fly up and away. Imbolondo gallops off one way and the startled herd of animals we've been walking alongside start to stampede away in two different directions. Two lionesses attack the youngest of the animals from behind while another ambushes the herd from the side. The lion moves into the kill after the lionesses have done most of the chasing and have brought down a young wildebeest. Imbolondo carries us to a safe distance and we stop to watch what is happening.

"It's the nature of lions to stay by their kill and eat until they are full," Imbolondo says. "Then it's their nature to sleep. It's the nature of lions to have their own hunting grounds so now we can travel on feeling that we are safer from lion attack for a while."

I'm wondering if it's possible to choose to have a different nature from the one I was given at my birth. Chibwe is thinking

Dust and Rain

the same. I wonder if we would choose to have similar natures
to each other.

CHAPTER TEN
THE NATURE OF PEOPLE

Time doesn't matter to Imbolondo, but time still matters to me and Chibwe. One reason is that even though we are omnivores, we are tired of eating dried fish and roast maize cobs. In any case we don't have much of that food left in our bags. Desperate for a new fresh taste, I pick some of the same bush fruit that I told Masika to try eating for vitamins and, just as I warned him it would, it gives us both sore stomachs.

I pick herbs that Chibwe and I can rub on our skin to keep away tsetse flies because they give us such painful bites. Soon after that we find a hole by a river where elephants have been wallowing and we throw mud at each other until we are covered with sticky clay. It's fun, but we're even happier when Imbolondo takes as to a clear rocky pool where we can swim and wash ourselves without being eaten by crocodiles.

In spite of our distrust of crocodiles, we observe crocodile mothers caring for their eggs and babies in a wide river. This same wide river disappears underground under a ridge of granite rocks and only wells up again miles further away. We examine termites making their giant air-cooled castles and farming their fungi. We avoid ants in a huge hissing army who eat everything alive that crosses their path. We see summer squirrels, banded mongooses, blue-headed lizards and diamond-patterned snakes. We watch great flocks of birds wheeling overhead as well as tiny solitary birds hiding in bushes. We make friends with chameleons and millipedes. We are fascinated by marsh harriers fluttering over the grasslands in the evening like giant hawk-moths and we see butterflies, moths and caterpillars of all sizes and colours everywhere. We see and hear so many different kinds of insects and spiders that we can't give them all names.

"It's the nature of all creatures to need water and plants," Imbolondo says often to us. "It's the nature of plants to need creatures and water."

"Water is life!" Chibwe and I repeat back to him. "That's what Ma told us!"

One night Imbolondo takes us through the dry miombo forests where the sound of bees and the making of honey never stops.

"It's the nature of African bees to guard their honey" he says. "It's the nature of bees to sting intruders and honey thieves. We will go quietly and quickly through the forests at night while they are resting but we will ask a honey badger to fetch us a honey comb tomorrow. I know that you children are tired of dried fish and want something sweet!"

"It's the nature of children to like sweet honey," Chibwe and I say, laughing.

"Now children," Imbolondo asks us. "Have you begun to understand what your natures are?"

Chibwe and I look at each other and then we hang our heads. Neither of us want to answer. I give Chibwe a nudge with my elbow.

"We aren't sure of the answer," Chibwe tries to explain. "We don't know if all people have the same nature as each other in the same way that ants and insects behave in the same way as each other. Perhaps people can all choose to be different?"

"We know that we can choose to be good or bad people," I say in a rush. "We know that we should treat other people with kindness and respect but sometimes the things we think are good, don't turn out good or right."

Chibwe nods, "If we were like animals and just obeyed our nature then nothing would be our fault or our responsibility. The trouble is we aren't all wise and we can't all be clever."

"Sometimes right things go wrong," I say. "Sometimes we make mistakes."

"We must still do the right thing," Chibwe says, and this time I nod. "If we know what it is!"

"But we do know what's right – most of the time – don't we?" I answer, feeling cross and confused. "I want to do what's right – I think that is the nature of most people, but if that's true why are there people like Mr Wabenzi, Ma Richwoman and Pa Badman doing bad things?"

"If you start to do wrong things then its hard to go back and make them right, I think,." Chibwe suggests.

"Do you think that Pa did something wrong that helped to make the drought in the Valley? Do you think Malasha shouldn't cut down trees to make charcoal?" I ask.

"Can Makemba help us get rid of Kambili and end the drought? What if we can't even find her?" Chibwe asks. That's when we realise that the two of us are talking to each other and Imbolondo is not saying anything or even listening to us.

"What do you think we should do Imbolondo?" Chibwe asks him.

"Questions! Questions!" Imbolondo snorts and humps up his shoulder.

"It's the nature of humans and animals and plants to adapt to changes and solve problems. Humans are different. It's the nature of humans to ask questions. It's the nature of humans to make choices. Humans can choose to make changes to the world. Humans can choose to hurt the world or they can choose to care for it and all the animals and plants that live on it," Imbolondo answers. "If that is your nature, then it's time for you to carry on with your search for Makemba and ask her questions about how to choose to make the right changes. Tomorrow we will reach the Evergreen Forest and there we will part."

CHAPTER ELEVEN
THE EVERGREEN FOREST

Early the next morning we come to the edge of the High Savannah and we look down across a vast forest that stretches all the way to the distant horizon.

"I'll carry you down to where the forest begins," Imbolondo says.

"From there you must make your own way on foot. I can't tell you where to go or what to do. As there is no grass in the Evergreen Forest, there is nothing for me to eat. It is not in my nature to eat the leaves of forest trees so I must return home to Chief Ikabonga's village and the Great River."

When we reach the edge of the Forest, Chibwe and I wrap our arms around as much of Imbolondo's great neck as we can reach.

"Thank you Imbolondo," we say. "We could never have come here without your help. We will never forget you and your strength and wise advice."

"Don't be afraid Chibwe and Chipo. It is your nature to be brave and resourceful. You will find a way to defeat the Drought Witch whatever happens to you here in the Evergreen Forest."

Imbolondo turns around to leave us then he stops and speaks to us for the last time.

"It is the nature of monkeys and apes to eat food that is also safe for the stomachs of children. It is the nature of children and monkeys to climb trees."

Chibwe and I watch Imbolondo canter away from us. I have never felt so lonely and abandoned as I do now and I know that Chibwe feels the same as me.

"Well, my sister," Chibwe says. "Shall we go and look for monkey food?"

"Yes, my brother. Let's do that," I answer.

It's in our nature to care for each other but sometimes it's been hard to know what was the best way to do that. Once Chibwe thought it was best to leave me behind. Since then I've often wished he had or that I had stayed at home.

We have to go in single file through the thick undergrowth and the trunks of crowded trees in the Evergreen Forest. We go slowly and carefully, looking and listening. Forests are strange for us and we don't know what kinds of creatures live there or what dangers we may meet.

"Where do you think we will find Makemba?" I ask Chibwe. He hesitates, then answers.

"I don't really know but I think she must live at the heart of the Evergreen Forest."

"Is that the middle of the Forest or the most important place in it?" I persist.

Chibwe stops. I wonder if I've annoyed him but I carry on.

"I mean we don't know how big the forest is and it's even easier to get lost and go in circles, isn't it? The ground is all shadowed and sometimes we can't even see the sun or sky."

"You are right, Chipo," Chibwe says. "You often are. Makemba is the Wise Womn of the Garden and we've been told that we'll find her at the Source of the Great River. That must be the Heart we're looking for – the Heart is where the Great River begins – and that is what we have to find."

"But where - - but how?" I start to say, but Chibwe is looking up at the trees and thinking aloud.

"I must find the tallest tree and climb up to where I can see for the greatest distance. If Imbolondo carried us across the high savannah east alongside the Great River then I may be able to see where the Great River flows out of the Evergreen Forest in the west. If we can walk through the forest in that direction until we find the Great River then all we need to do is walk upstream till we find Makemba."

"Is that all!" I say wishing I could easily climb up a tree and walk across the roof of the forest. I have a crick in my neck from staring up and I can see that the tallest trees don't have many branches to hold onto. "It won't be easy."

"No, it won't!" says Chibwe, looking at me. I hope he's not thinking of leaving me behind again. "Wait here, Chipo, with our food bag and water until I come down again from this tree." Before I can say anything Chibwe is climbing up the nearest and tallest mundane tree and I'm sitting at the bottom worrying about the rustling sounds that I can hear around me in the forest.

I've got my back to the tree trunk but I know which branch I can grab first. If I have to climb up the tree in a hurry, I'll drop everything and go. The small duiker that appears is as nervous as I feel. She has a rounded back from ducking and hiding and a yellow splodge on her spine like a permanent patch of sunlight. She carries her head low and her eyes blink shyly into slits. I'm keeping as still as possible watching her searching for food when the sky overhead explodes into screeches and falling fruit and she vanishes without a sound. Chibwe jumps down beside me doubled up with laughter.

"I annoyed some monkeys," he says, grinning. "They were eating fruit when they saw me. Now they've thrown it at me. Let's eat – I'm hungry!"

We gather up what we can. There isn't much and some of it is squashed or rotten but still it's food and its juicy purple plums taste as sweet as honey.

"I've seen some rocky hills that stick up high above the forest and I've noticed some tall trees that we can use as landmarks on our route," Chibwe says after we've finished the fruit. "We'll aim in that direction and I'll climb trees every now and then to see if we're still going the right way."

"We're going to need to find something to eat, Chibwe," I say. "What do you think we can find here? We also need to find water. This forest is dry and I haven't seen any streams."

"We'll look out as we go," Chibwe says. "We've a couple of dried fish left and the water bottle is full."

"We'll be running out of matches soon," I say. "We need to save them for an emergency."

Chibwe is silent. We haven't made many fires because we don't have any food to cook. We set off walking through the trees. We try to go as straight as we can but the trees don't get out of our way so we have to keep twisting round them and it's slow going. I soon feel tired.

Our journey feels never-ending. The nights are long and dark and it's difficult to find good places to sleep. Chibwe wants us to sleep in the trees if we can find a branch that's broad and comfortable enough for one of us at least to get some sleep. We try different solutions.

"You go up first, Chipo, and I'll keep watch on the ground first. Then we'll change places," Chibwe says.

I know he's trying to protect me. It works for a few nights but I have less and less energy for climbing up trees. One night I fall out of the tree and wake up Chibwe who's fallen asleep on the ground instead of staying on guard. I don't break any bones or hurt myself much. Fortunately, I don't land on Chibwe, though I do give him a terrible fright.

"I thought you were a leopard," he says breathlessly.

We're too tired to laugh and even too tired to be cross with each other.

"We need to eat some meat," Chibwe says. "It will give us energy."

"How do we get meat?" I ask. "If we set a trap then we have to keep coming back to it instead of looking for the river."

"Perhaps we'll find more eggs on the way," Chibwe says.

We robbed a crested guinea fowl nest of all its eggs and ate them raw a few days ago.

"They're probably better for us if they're turning into chicks," Chibwe says. "More protein."

They don't begin to fill my empty tummy but I feel a little less tired. We eat fruit if we can reach it easily. Climbing a tree feels as if we're adding miles onto our journey. We collect some mopane worms, a few grasshoppers, and a couple of cicadas. It's not worth cooking them so we let them dry and then eat them one by one as we walk. I'm beginning to stumble more often.

We find ourselves under a Raining Tree. Its leaves are covered with holes made by tiny insects who live in bubbles of froth. The insects rain down pure water sucked from the tree and leave puddles of clear water that we can drink from on the ground.

"Should we stay here, Chibwe?" I ask. "At least we won't be thirsty."

"We won't find Makemba if we stay here," Chibwe answers. "One day the insects in the tree will fly away and no more rain will fall from the leaves."

We're too tired to worry about wild animals. When we bump into some wild pigs, Chibwe shouts at them and they run away. They're all females and have no piglets with them, otherwise they might have chased us. They leave behind some roots they've dug up and we decide we can risk chewing them. We also find some chanterelle mushrooms nearby that taste delicious. Water is our biggest problem. We chew the few stems of grass we find for a bit of moisture and lick the dew off leaves. One night it rains but it's hard to collect falling rain in a water bottle. Luckily, we were asleep on a bed of thick moss on the night it rained and we squeeze some water out of the moss and into our bottle.

"It's not enough," Chibwe says. "We must find a stream."

Chibwe's eyes look dull and his skin is greyish and slack

but that might be because my eyes are growing foggy.

"Do you remember when we left home?" I ask Chibwe. "When are we going back?"

"Home?" Chibwe says. "It's so long ago. Why did we leave home?"

"There's something we're supposed to be doing because of home – isn't there?" I say.

"We've got to find water," Chibwe says. "We must keep going on."

"I need to rest, Chibwe," I say. "Chipo must sleep." If I don't say my name, I won't even remember who I am.

"Okay," says Chibwe. His head is on his arms and his arms are wrapped around his knees and he is slipping over onto his side.

"Okay," I say, and I crawl close to him and sleep too.

I think we will sleep for ever.

***

Perhaps we slept all night. Perhaps it was only a few hours. When I wake up it's daylight and what I hear is a sound like water being poured out of our water-bottle into a cup.

"phug-a-fug-a-shug-a-thug-a-glug-GLUG"

It's a beautiful sound. I lie there enjoying it.

"phug-a-fug-a-shug-a-thug-a-glug-GLUG"

I think Chibwe is awake too.

"Do you hear that?" I ask.

"Yes," he says. "It's a rain-bird calling us."

"We'd better follow it then," I say. "Where is it going to take us?"

When I stand up, I feel light and my arms and legs don't seem to be attached to my body.

"Are you awake, Chibwe?" I ask.

"I think so," he says as he staggers to his feet. "We mustn't forget our bag."

The rain-bird sounds as if it's moving further away from us down a sloping path.

"phug-a-fug-a-shug-a-thug-a-glug-GLUG," it calls again.

We follow it down the path but we never seem get any closer to it. I'm floating but Chibwe walks as if he's still asleep and can't feel his feet. I don't know if we walk for a short time or a long time but when we arrive at the end of the path, we see, perched on a branch over a narrow stream of sparkling water, the rain-bird bowing its head and calling to us. Immediately we both kneel down and drink and drink and drink and splash water over our faces.

"Thank you rain-bird," we keep on saying.

"phug-a-fug-a-shug-a-thug-a-glug-GLUG," it answers and flies away.

There are some edible green leaves at the water's edge with bitter roots that we nibble. The sharp taste makes me feel awake.

"Where do we go to now Chibwe?" I ask. "I think I remember what we must do."

"So do I," Chibwe says. "First we must find something to eat."

Chibwe stands up to look around and we both hear two short bird whistles, one high and one low and a small brown and white bird darts to a branch just by Chibwe's shoulder.

"Hello honey guide," I say. "Please take us to a beehive and some honey."

The honey guide looks at me first out of one eye, then out of the other. He whistles, flies on a short way and waits for us. Chibwe and I whistle back and follow him, deeper and deeper, whistle after whistle, flight after short flight, up the narrow stream into the Evergreen Forest. We're not thirsty any more but we are hungry and honey is what we need and want.

The forest is thicker, the trees are bigger and the shade is darker. The honey guide whistles twice more and flies up high onto a branch.

"I can hear the bees buzzing," I say. "The hive must be very high up in this tree."

Chibwe and I are both standing on tiptoe looking up at the honey guide.

"I think it must be at the top of this huge fig tree in front of us," Chibwe says. He reaches out to find a handhold on the trunk when the whole tree shifts and shakes and the honey guide whistles and flaps its wings.

Chibwe and I step back in alarm. The honey guide is not perching on a branch but on the shoulder of an immensely tall and handsome woman. She is wearing a skirt of bark-cloth and is decorated with necklaces and bangles of flowers, seeds and pods. Her skin is green and her hair is moving and waving like grass in the wind. I think I can see it growing as I watch.

"Greetings, Chibwe and Chipo," she says. "I am Makemba, the Wise Woman of the Garden and you have come to my home at the Source of the Great River."

Then Makemba kneels down and takes us both in her arms and we know with great happiness that we have returned to the roots of our existence and found peace.

"A river that forgets its source will dry up," Makemba says.

"A people that forget their roots will not be able to survive.

You have found your roots. You have found the source of the Great River."

CHAPTER TWELVE
MAKEMBA, THE WISE WOMAN OF THE GARDEN

Chibwe and I sleep and eat and sleep again. Makemba herself brings us food and drink. As first we can only swallow honeyed fruit-flavoured water and we're too tired and too hungry to sleep for long. Gradually as we eat more solid foods, we sleep for longer periods suspended in two woven hammocks in the fig tree. We're comfortable and safe as we haven't been since Kambili arrived at the Farm in the Valley. Though we don't remember it, we must also have bathed or washed because we find we're clean and we feel good. The food we eat is varied and delicious in its flavours and textures. It's a feast of different colours for the eyes too. There's yellow maize, white cassava, brown millet and sorghum, orange groundnuts, green kale, spikey lemon cucumbers and red tomatoes. We eat fish and crayfish and bite into succulent and chewy meat. The air is full of soothing and melodious sounds day and night. Birds, bees and insects chorus, chirrup, churr and buzz around us and Makemba sings as she works. We begin to feel strong and well again.

"How long have we been here?" I ask Chibwe when I wake up one morning.

"I've no idea," Chibwe says. "We'll have to ask Makemba."

"How long has it taken us to get here?" I ask. "It feels like a very long time since we saw Ma and Pa."

Chibwe sighs.

"I'm so worried about Ma and Pa," he says. "We must get back to them soon. When we were starving in the Evergreen Forest, we didn't think of them or their names;"

I don't like to think about that time when I didn't even know who I was.

"Makemba will help us," I say confidently. "I do trust Makemba. She must have some magic that will break Kambili's spell. Do you think she'll come with us and use her magic when we get home?"

"I don't think we can find the way home without help," Chibwe says. "We've done it though! We've got here! It must be all right from now on."

That's when I get a nervous fluttering in my stomach.

"Will Makemba come home with us? Will it really be all right at last?"

We scramble out of our hammocks, climb down the fig tree and go and look for Makemba. All we have to do is follow the sound of her singing.

"Good morning, Makemba," Chibwe says. "We've come to thank you for looking after us and making us well again."

Makemba bends down low until she can look into our eyes.

"So, children, now that you are well at last, are you ready to start the work you need to do?"

Chibwe and I look at each other and then we nod our heads.

"We think so," Chibwe says. "We're in your debt."

Makemba laughs and the sound of her laughter is like sunshine after a rainstorm and like a rainstorm after hot weather.

"We are all in debt to the world around us that gives us life and air and water and food," she says. "This is a gift that's given to all of us and it is a gift that we must share with all people."

"I know why you are here, Chibwe and Chipo. You have come to ask me to help you get rid of Kambili the Drought Witch. There is no magic that can do that and so it's not in my power at all. The Drought Witch gets her power from the greedy, careless behaviour of people who do not care for the land and the trees and the rivers that make life possible."

"What can we do then? What can we do?" I cry.

I'm so upset that I burst into tears and throw myself in a despairing heap on the ground.

"Chipo!" Makemba says sternly. "Can you cry enough tears to end the drought? Think of your brother! Perhaps he needs your help?"

Chibwe crouches beside me and pats my shoulder.

"Chipo! Come on. Get up! We have work to do here. We have to start somewhere."

Makemba laughs again but it doesn't sound unkind. I sit up snivelling and wipe my face.

"Chibwe and Chipo, you have come so far and done so much and learned so many things. Come down to the Source of the Great River and we'll talk about what two children can do to end the drought."

Makemba sits down under the fig tree and we make ourselves comfortable by her feet.

"Begin your stories Chipo and Chibwe," Makemba says. "Tell me what happened to you and what have you learned on your journey to find me."

"If there is no rain, we can't grow any food," I say. "That's what happened to Ma and Pa and our farm in the Valley after Kambili, the Drought Witch arrived."

"There are some very bad people in the world like Mr Wabenzi, Ma Richwoman and Pa Badman," Chibwe says. "And some very good people like Aunt Chimunya, David, Isaac and Palma, and Winnie and Wally."

"And many more people who are sometimes good and sometimes not very good," I say. "We don't understand what makes droughts happen and we don't know what people can do to stop droughts happening. We don't know if droughts happen because people are bad or if they make mistakes. Perhaps droughts happen anyway by chance?"

"There are traditional people like Malasha who understand the wilderness but who cut down trees for charcoal. His time is past maybe? There are also city people who don't understand the wilderness and cut down all the trees so they can cook food," Chibwe says. "There are people who only want to make money for themselves and there are people who want to make the world a better place."

"People need food. They must grow it or buy it and then they must cook it so they need fire or electricity," I say. "We need gardens so we can grow our food, but without rain it isn't possible."

Chibwe and I look at each other and together we ask Makemba,

"Makemba, you are the Wise Women of the Garden, please

tell us how we can end the drought and once again grow food in our gardens. What are we doing wrong? What are we doing that has brought Kambili, the Drought Witch, into our lives to punish us?"

Makemba is silent for a while. At last she stands up, picks us up and sits us on her shoulders so we are among the branches of the forest trees.

"Look around you at the Evergreen Forest, children," she says. "For thousands of years the people of the earth have lived in gardens and used them for food and shelter. So too, have animals, birds and insects. Gardens shape people and all the creatures. Creatures and people shape gardens. People shape the wildernesses too. People and animals live together and make use of each other. Now, however, people have begun to destroy the wildernesses and the gardens that give them life even though they know that life is not possible without them. People have forgotten that they are part of the natural world. People have forgotten that they cannot live without the natural world. They belong to it but it does not belong to them alone, but to all creatures."

Makemba reaches up into the top branches of a giant fig tree. It is full of chatter and noise and songs from birds and monkeys. She picks some figs and gives them to Chibwe and me.

"Understand the giant fig tree," Makemba says. "It feeds green pigeons, monkeys, baboons and many different creatures including human beings. It depends on tiny wasps to fertilise it and make its fruit ripe and sweet. It can grow even on a rocky cliff. Its roots reach deep and far. It can begin its life on a high branch of a tall tree in the forest and become the biggest tree of all. Trees help all creatures breathe. We must have trees to live. In the Evergreen Forest there are all kinds of plants and animals, birds, and insects that live together. Without the trees and the plants there would be no food for the creatures of the forest. Plants and trees, however, also make use of the creatures and people. Insects and bees fertilise the flowers and make the seeds so that trees and plants can grow again. Some of the seeds of the plants are carried by the birds and animals to new places where they can grow. Trees and plants use the dung of animals to help themselves grow strong and well. Plants are older and wiser than people. They have found ways of living and growing in deserts and in water, in cold and hot countries and everywhere they make the air that people need to be able to breathe."

Makemba lifted us from her shoulders and put us down onto the ground.

"Watch what I do," she says. "Learn about the earth under our feet."

Makemba scoops up the earth of the forest floor in her giant green hands. She makes it into a ball with water from the Source of the River then with one swift movement she flings it onto the ground. The earth ball shatters into many fragments and dries quickly into dust which Makemba blows away with one strong blow of her breath.

"The earth of the forest is poor and fragile. There is no richness in it," she explains to us. "But the forest trees know how to live on such poor soil and how to give shelter to many other creatures as well. The forest trees can even survive fires and grow again. If you cut down the forest, however, the soil that's left behind can't grow food and there will be less good air for people to breathe."

"I've seen farmers who grow food on soil like that after they've cut down all the trees," Chibwe says. "Pa says they have to use very expensive and poisonous chemicals to make plants grow and they have to use them every year."

"He is right," Makemba says. "What grows on those fields after the crops have been harvested, Chibwe?"

"Some weeds do grow but they die soon without rain. They don't feed birds or animals for long. Then the earth turns to dust and blows away just as you showed us," Chibwe answers.

"The soil of the earth can't, on its own, make air for us to breathe and give us the moisture that helps make the rain we need for food to grow either. It is trees and plants that protect the earth from becoming too hot and too dry. Trees and plants help to give us rain," Makemba says. "Watch again."

Once more Makemba scoops up a ball of earth but this time it is from her own garden. Once more, she shapes it into a ball with water from the Source of the Great River. Once more, Makemba flings the earth ball onto the ground but this time the ball does not shatter. Instead it flattens into a round pancake. It's a dark moist colour. We each take turns to try blow it away but it can't be done and we both end up laughing and breathless.

"I've looked after the earth of my garden," Makemba tells us. "I've fed it with animal dung and leaf mould. This earth is rich in everything that plants need to grow well. I've kept my garden covered with growing vegetation. I've stopped it from getting dry. Every season it gives me and my animals both food and pleasure. It is a home for bees, insects and birds. Together, we all share my garden. No garden and no wilderness make a home for only one creature or one plant or a single person. Without sharing, the earth can't provide food or air for us."

"Please, can you teach us how to make a garden like yours and how to farm so that we look after the earth, Makemba?" Chibwe asks and Makemba smiles at him.

"You'll make a good farmer, Chibwe, and feed many people."

I'm still worried. There is something more that I need to understand. It's something that both Grandmother and my mother often talked about in the past. It's something to do with the Rain Spirits but Grandmother says that it's only possible to speak to the Spirits if someone who has special spirit medium powers asks them to visit us. I think we need the spirit medium powers to bring the Rain Spirits.

"Makemba, we need to look after the earth but we need to understand where the rain comes from too," I say. "Do we need a spirit medim to ask for the Rain Spirits to come back to us? Please, tell me all about them?"

Makemba looks at me.

"Yes, Chipo. We do need to understand the Rain Spirits. We'll have to go on a journey to find them but this time we can't travel with our bodies so we need somebody who is connected with the Spirits and who has the gift of speaking with them to take us to the Rain Spirits."

I frown. "Where can we find somebody like that?" I ask.

Makemba and Chibwe are both looking at me. I can hear my own breath and every beat of my heart, then both sounds stop and I hear a long moment of silence.

"You are the one the Spirits talk to, Chipo." Chibwe says

"It takes courage to visit the place of Spirits." Makemba says and she bends down so she can look right into my eyes. "You are a child, Chipo. If you go on this journey, it must be your choice alone. It's hard and it's dangerous to use such extraordinary power when you are so young."

I need to think first. I walk away from Chibwe and Makemba and I go to the Source of the Great River and kneel down. I put my hands into the clear water and let it run like silk over my fingers. I splash its coolness onto my face. I make my hands into a cup and drink from it. I feel refreshed and strong again.

I remember Ma's words, "Water is Life."

I stand up and walk back to Makemba and Chibwe.

"I'm ready," I say. "What must I do?"

CHAPTER THIRTEEN
THE RAIN SPIRITS

Makemba and Chibwe come with me to the Source of the Great River and sit down on either side of me holding my hands. My brother's hand is warm and friendly. Makemba's hand feels like the lithe green branches of a tree and her body feels like a great tree trunk I can rest against without falling.

"Close your eyes, Chipo," Makemba says. "This can't be made to happen by wanting it to happen. It happens only when you trust the Rain Spirits. It happens outside of time and space."

Makemba is right.

I wait until I feel the Rain Spirits around me and that's when I know I must give them my trust. I feel myself reaching out to them like a baby bird taking its first flight away from its nest.

Nothing that happens after that can be described using ordinary words but ordinary words are all I have. When it's all over, Chibwe asks me to tell him what it felt like. First, he tells me what he saw happen to me.

"Your body went all stiff as if it had turned into metal," Chibwe says. "Your eyes were strange. I couldn't see you in them any more. I could see the sky. Then you began to shiver as if you had the worst malaria fever ever. Next you began to shake so hard I thought that you would break into tiny pieces. Then you felt hollow and very light like a husk when the seed has gone but still as if you were made of something like steel. After that you were quiet and didn't move at all. Makemba and

I just sat beside you for a very long time – it felt like days and days and nights and nights but maybe it was seconds only because we were outside of time."

I search for the words I can use. I need new words for things that I've never seen and never knew existed in the world.

"I was at the centre of a great storm of huge power. At first all the movement and energy were outside of me but then that changed and I, myself, became the power. It was as if I was both thunder and lightning but I wasn't the thunder and lightning of one storm, but of every storm everywhere that ever happened in the whole world. I stopped being myself, just one small girl, called Chipo. I was the maker of the power and I was the power itself. Then I was dissolving, and dissolving as if I was rain raining upwards through all the storms into the vastness of the sky."

I stop explaining for a few minutes because the remembering is so sharp and so powerful that I feel as if it is happening twice to me. Chibwe listens patiently, but Makemba listens as if I am reminding her of things that also happened to her. Her great hands comfort me so I know I've come safely back to the ground again.

I continue, "When I'm in the sky, I'm the whole sky because I am water mixed with air. I am raindrops and I am rain frozen into hailstones. I'm such fine moisture that I float away into clouds, drift into cloud banks, and boil up into thunderheads bursting with rainstorms. I change into a billion-trillion different snowflakes and I fall softly down and down. Then I spin into blizzards of ice and snow. I'm solid again but I'm frozen into solid ice. I'm as huge as icebergs and as brittle as icicles. I melt away and I cover the sea and I taste salt. I evaporate and rise upwards again. I dissolve into mists and then I become dancing rainbows reflecting sunshine and changing – all the time I'm changing. Sometimes I'm the size and shape of mountains – sometimes I am as tiny as a single minute molecule."

I have to stop again and rest. The Rain Spirits took me so far and so high and so low that I've been everywhere in the whole wide world.

"I've been tornadoes, I've been hurricanes, I've been cyclones. I've raced across the seas and blown the seas into great rolling waves and sent them crashing on far distant shores. I've poured myself constantly over rainforests, and flooded into valleys and washed away homes and trees and living creatures. I've soared over deserts that were too hot for me to touch and I've risen up in spiralling thermals over steamy cities and lakes carrying birds of prey, cranes, kites and eagles up high with me."

"I've soaked into the ground down into underground caverns and tumbled out again over cliffs and rocks and I've flowed out into the sea. I'm always moving. Trees suck me up through their roots and breathe me out again into the air. I float and I fly and I am the sky."

Makemba's hands support me. Chibwe's hand squeezes mine.

"The wind carries me – but I am rain and I move the winds also – we are together, wind, weather and rain. The winds tumble and twist, and bend around the world. They race to destroy with their gales and they soothe gently with their breezes. They blow all around the world carrying me – carrying rain – carrying moisture and water and giving it to the earth as falling raindrops so that plants can grow and rivers can run and seas and lakes can live and be full of fish and so that the earth can have people and animals and gardens and food on it."

I'm so tired by now, that I don't know if I can carry on speaking. It seems that the Rain Spirits haven't left me yet because my eyes keep filling with tears. I must finish telling Makemba and Chibwe about my journey so that I can sleep.

"I've been to places that won't have me. I've seen places that reject me. I've seen new deserts made by people that the Rain Spirits can no longer visit. Some of the deserts are made into stony craters by men who want to mine for minerals and precious stones – some are made of bare earth by the sun's heat. The gift that the Rain Spirits give to the rivers of the earth is blocked by dams and the gifts of moisture that trees give to the sky have been cut away. The waters that the Rain Spirits provide for fish and plants are being poisoned or polluted. There are droughts – more and more droughts, floods and landslides where trees have been cut down. There are places that the Rain Spirits cannot go to any more."

I'm crying again.

"The Rain Spirits need the earth. The earth needs the rain of the Rain Spirits. Something is wrong – something is missing from our world. It's a big and powerful word to use," I say.

"It's the word that can make all things better again," I tell Makemba and Chibwe.

"The Rain Spirits want to love the earth. The earth needs

the loving of the Rain Spirits. People need the Rain Spirits. People need to love their earth and their world. The word that everybody needs to use and to understand is Love. Love is what is needed to end all droughts."

"Are the Rain Spirits going to come and help us defeat Kambili?" Chibwe asks. He sounds very anxious to me.

"The Rain Spirits can only be what Rain Spirits are and obey the laws of the rain," I tell him. "We are the ones, the people, who must not drive the Rain Spirits away."

"We are the ones who must bring Love to the world."

Makemba picks me up in her cradling arms and carries me to my hammock in the trees so that I can rest and sleep.

I hear Chibwe say to Makemba, "We will find a way to defeat the Drought Witch! We must! We must find a way to love the earth and to respect the Rain Spirits."

I hear Makemba say to Chibwe.

"I will teach you both all that I know so that you can defeat Kambili."

I sleep at last.

CHAPTER FOURTEEN
MAKEMBA'S GARDEN

After I've recovered from my journey to the Rain Spirits, Makemba takes Chibwe and me into her garden to teach us how to make things grow.

"Some plants like each other but some plants are bad for each other. There are plants that are greedy and those that are generous. There are plants that feed from other plants and there are plants that support each other. All plants need light and air and water but there are plants that don't even need to put their roots into the earth," Makemba explains. "All of these things seem like magic but you can find them out for yourselves if you take the time to watch and learn.

"If you look carefully you can see that some plants reach out for each other. There are plants that are poisonous because they don't want to be eaten and plants that are delicious because they want to be eaten. There are plants that are pretty and plants that are perfumed so that they will attract insects and birds."

Chibwe and I spend days in Makemba's garden. We dig and we plant and we smell and we taste. We find plants that sting us and others that we can use to soothe insect bites.

"The plants that interest me most are the plants that I can grow for food," Chibwe says.

"I like the plants that can be made into medicines and ointments," I say. "But really – I like them all."

"Perhaps you should study to be a botanist like Palma," Chibwe says to me, and I nod with pleasure at the idea.

"I love the way that a garden attracts many insects and birds to it because it has so many different plants," I say.

"I love the way bees collect nectar and pollen for honey but also help the plants make seeds," Chibwe says. "I love the seeds that we can cook and eat too!"

We both laugh. We love the food we eat from Makemba's garden.

"I wonder how Palma and Isaac and Masika are and if they've saved the Secret Wilderness in the Big City from Mr Wabenzi," I say.

"I hope we see them again one day," Chibwe says.

"I hope we never see Mr Wabenzi again!" I say.

***

We spend many days working in the garden until one day Makemba picks Chibwe and me up and sits us once again on her shoulders, so she can carry us around the Evergreen Forest. We are at just the right height to see what she sees and to hear all that she has to tell us. It is a strange journey. The trees don't step out of Makemba's path but neither do we feel the branches or the trees that are in our way touch us. I'm not sure whether the Evergreen Forest has become so thin and transparent that we can pass right through it, or if Makemba and Chibwe and me have become ghosts. I hear a sound like the humming and vibrating of soft rain as we move. While we are moving, Makemba collects seeds from the trees to give to us. They are solid and real when we touch them.

"We must collect seeds from all and every forest tree for you to take back to the Valley," Makemba says. "Every tree has its own unique seeds. None of them look exactly the same and each one grows in a different way and needs to be in its own best environment so it can grow well."

"Pa has taught me the names of many trees," Chibwe says, and he starts to tell us the names he knows for all the trees.

"Ma has taught me about the medicines that she makes from their leaves, roots and bark," I say and I tell Makemba and Chibwe which trees give medicine to cure headaches and which are good for healing fevers or sadness.

Makemba nods her head and her living, growing green hair wraps itself around us as she does so. Chibwe and I laugh because it is tickling us.

"There are trees that walk to make new baby trees. There are those who grow baby trees on their roots. Many trees make seeds that travel to new places so that they can grow well and not crowd out their parent trees. There are trees whose seeds are made to travel on the wind," Makemba explains. "Some are light, some have wings, some have silky, feathery parachutes, some twist and spiral away from the tree. Some seed pods have to be in hot sun, so they explode and scatter their seeds as far away as possible."

Makemba has made us a woven sack to put all the seeds in that we are collecting. We have to look at every one, feel it, sniff it, weigh it and remember its name and remember how it likes to be planted so that it can grow well.

"I do like doing this," I tell Chibwe.

"Me too!" He replies. "I'm sure that when I know all about trees it will make me better at growing food when we get back to the farm. I know that that one is an ebony tree with a strong black heart and this one is an ironwood and can break an axe blade."

"There are seeds that are carried away by animals," Makemba says. "Some seeds get eaten and then they are found much later in the animal's dung. There are seeds that are only free to grow when birds like hornbills have used their beaks to crack open the seed cases. There are seeds that can't begin to grow until the coldest winter weather splits its hard shell in half. There are seeds that know they have to wait for the summer rains to burst their skins before they can put down roots."

"What are we collecting these seeds for?" Chibwe asks Makemba.

"You must plant all these seeds on your way back home," Makemba tells us. "If you want to stop the drought and bring back the rains, if you want to stop the earth becoming too hot for things to grow then you need to plant trees."

"Oh!" Chibwe says.

"Oh!" I say.

We are quiet while we think about the task that Makemba has given us to do.

"How can we get the seeds to grow when there's no rain?" Chibwe asks.

"You'll carry some water with you from the Source of the Great River," Makemba tells us. "On top of every seed that you plant you must put a drop of water. The water from the Source of the Great River has magical powers that will help the seeds grow into trees even in places that are dry and hard."

"We'll try to do our best," I say to her.

Makemba's voice is as deep as a well when she tells us our last duty.

"Chipo and Chibwe," she says. "You must keep one last drop of water to throw at Kambili, the Drought Witch. One last drop of water from the Source of the Great River is all you need to destroy her."

Makemba lifts us back off her shoulders and onto the ground.

"It's time to have supper. Now," she says. "Tomorrow you will start on your journey home."

"How do we know where to go?" Chibwe asks Makemba.

"Mokoro will guide you," she says. "He will take you down the Great River in his dugout canoe."

I wonder how that can be possible. Here in the Evergreen Forest, the Source of the Great River is only the very beginning of a small and narrow stream that I can jump over. The place where the Great River becomes deep and wide to float a dugout canoe must be very far away.

Makemba kneels down by the Source of the Great River. At first I think that she's holding a small black wriggling fish in her hands then I see that the tiny fish has a woman's body and two twisting tails. Could it be a miniature Mama Wati? Makemba releases the little creature into the water and it vanishes.

"Go well my dear friend and companion," Makemba says.

PART FOUR

SEEDS AND WATER

CHAPTER ONE
MOKORO

There's a moment in the night when I'm aware of movement and a sound and vibration like humming bees or falling rain even though I'm still sleeping. Maybe I'm only dreaming that I'm on Makemba's shoulders again and travelling swiftly through the Evergreen Forest. Whatever is happening to me it's pleasant and I feel safe. After a while I feel the warmth of the early morning sun on my face and the bright sunlight on my eyelids makes them blink and open. Chibwe and I are once again standing on the banks of the Great River. At our feet is a woven bag holding hundreds of seeds of all colours, shapes and sizes. Some shine, some are dull, and every one of them is carrying the possibility of becoming a new living and breathing tree. Our water bottle rests heavily against a bundle of food and fruit next to the bag of seeds.

The river is flowing gently past us through grass and woodland and a dugout canoe made from a whole tree trunk is resting on a sandbank in front of us. An extremely thin and tall man, standing on one leg and balanced by the pole in his hand, is looking away from us down the river. A fishlike black shape rises out of the water, raises a hand or a fin to the man as if to say goodbye before diving away under the surface. I wonder sleepily if Mama Wati has many sisters of different sizes or is always everywhere in rivers and can be any size that she needs to be.

As I feel more awake, I know something is missing. Someone of great importance is not to be seen. She isn't here with us.

"Makemba!" I call. "Makemba – where are you?"

I feel a huge dark hole has opened up in the middle of me because I'm so sad and lonely.

"Makemba don't leave us! Makemba."

I run to Chibwe and we put our arms around each other. I'm trying hard not to cry. At least I have Chibwe, and we have each other and all the seeds and an important task to do. But I want to see Makemba and say goodbye to her before we part. Leaving Makemba and the Evergreen Forest and Makemba's garden is so painful.

Before I despair, I hear Makemba's laugh and so does Chibwe. I look up and around and feel the powerful and comforting hold of her green and growing hands and arms encircling both of us.

"Chipo and Chibwe, I'll never leave you," Makemba's voice says. "I'm always with you. I'm always with gardeners and farmers and all those who love and care for growing things. I'm in each seed you plant and everything you grow and care for and love – I'm in your hearts and you are in mine forever."

"I love you, Makemba!" I call

"I love you, Makemba!" echoes Chibwe.

"We love you, Makemba!" we say together and at that moment we see the shivering transparency of Makemba's presence in everything around us and know she will be with us always.

***

The tall, thin man by the water's edge turns his head around like a bird so he can see us face to face. He beckons to us to come and get into his dugout canoe.

"Hello," Chibwe says to him. "You must be Mokoro. I'm Chibwe and this is my sister, Chipo."

Mokoro shakes his head once in answer to the question, once in greeting to Chibwe and once to me. He points at our bags of seeds and food and waves his hand at the dugout canoe.

"I don't think he talks much," Chibwe says. "Let's get into the dugout canoe and see what happens next."

Mokoro smiles when we do as he indicates. He has a wide mouth and we can see that every one of his teeth has been filed and shaped into a sharp point. I wonder why they're like that but as he doesn't talk, he won't tell me if I ask him.

As soon as we are seated and our bags are safely stowed in the dugout canoe, Mokoro pushes it out into the river and vaults skilfully onto the end of it with his pole. After that he uses the pole to keep the boat going in the right direction and to steer us away from the river banks or floating islands of grass and weed. We move with noiseless smoothness at the speed of the river's current while the life of all the river creatures carries on around us, untroubled by our passing. Chibwe and I have nothing to do but look and wonder. There are places where the river water is so clear that we can watch the fish underneath us and see the plants and creatures that live on the bottom of the river. We slide over a crocodile, lying motionless below us. It's longer than the dugout canoe and its belly is much wider.

"Look at the size of that crocodile!" Chibwe says. "We could all fit inside it – you, me and Mokoro too!"

"Where are we going to sleep at night?" I say feeling worried. "We won't be safe from crocodiles on the banks and there are no trees to climb."

We stop before the sky begins to get dark. Mokoro hops into the river with his pole and a fishing net. After a short time, he brings us back some fresh fish which we grill on a small fire for supper. After we've all eaten, Mokoro makes us a bed in the canoe on top of his fishing nets which are somehow already dry. I find some herbs to rub on our skin to keep the mosquitoes away.

"Otherwise we won't sleep at all!" I say.

"It makes us smell horrid!" Chibwe says wrinkling his nose. "But anything is better than mosquito bites. Where is Mokoro going to sleep?"

"Mokoro doesn't seem to need to sleep or lie down," I say after I've watched him standing by the canoe. "I think he lets one half of his body sleep for a while and then he lets the other half sleep. First, he shuts one eye and stands on one leg, then he shuts the other eye and stands on the other leg."

Chibwe and I try to watch Mokoro but in the end we fall asleep. When we wake up next morning he is still there, standing on one leg with one eye open.

"He doesn't seem to be at all tired," I say.

"And we haven't been eaten by crocodiles either," Chibwe replies.

We set off again on our quiet journey with Mokoro, our

silent guide, and we hear around us the sounds and the music of the river, the splashes as small creatures leap into the water, the rustles as something scurries off the banks, the plop as a monitor lizard goes for a swim, the insistent noise of the frogs. We listen to the calls and cries of startled birds as we pass by and the songs of those reed birds who are courting or building nests. We look into the eyes of antelope drinking at the water's edge and once we stare straight into the dripping mouth of a thirsty lion. Mokoro makes his way carefully around pods of hippos in the river and he keeps away from the river banks where crocodiles sun themselves with their tongue-less mouths gaping open.

Every evening Mokoro catches fish for supper. Every night we sleep in the dugout canoe while Mokoro keeps watch. Some nights we can swim in the shallow water of a sandy bank and sometimes we can run and play on an open grassy stretch of land. We talk to each other about what we must do next.

"Do you know how far away home is?" I ask Chibwe. "Do you know how long the Great River is? Do you know when we'll get there?"

Chibwe shakes his head and frowns as he tries to work it out.

"Do you remember how many days it took us to travel from the minibus accident with Winnie and Wally?" he asks. He looks at his fingers for a moment and then curls them into fists. Counting fingers isn't going to help us much.

"We spent a day walking across the flood plains. We were at the fishing village for a while and then we were on Imbolondo's back for ages. I can't remember how long we were lost in the Evergreen Forest and I don't know if it's possible to count the time we spent in Makemba's garden at the Source of the Great River. If we could remember exactly that's roughly how long it would take us to get to the Small Town on the Great River."

We have no answers and in any case that's not all we have to think about.

"Will Mokoro leave us at the Small Town?" I ask Chibwe. "We've got no money for a minibus journey and I don't want to go back to the Big City in case Ma Richwoman or Mr Wabenzi find us there."

Chibwe just shakes his head.

"I think we must have been away from home for the whole season of the hot weather," he says. "It's starting to get cooler at nights and the darkness is falling faster."

Neither of us mention Ma and Pa though both of us think about them all the time.

"Do you think we might get news about the drought in the Valley when we reach the Small Town?" I say. "Somebody there will have a television or a radio."

"Do you think people in the Small Town will help us?" I ask.

"Some will and some won't," Chibwe answers, but I knew that already.

***

One day we see, in the faraway distance, a thin dark line of smoke rising into the sky. A little further on we think we can almost hear voices. Mokoro's head turns in that direction and both his eyes open, but he poles us along much more slowly and we edge in closer to the bank.

"Look!" Chibwe says. "There are cattle on the bank."

"Perhaps we're near a village," I say, hoping.

My stomach skips and dances in excitement. I would love to be with other children again so that I can play games with some girls my age and we can tell each other secrets. It's at that moment that Chibwe and I hear a familiar deep and very low voice.

"Hello children." says Imbolondo. "I've been expecting you to return to Ikabonga's village for some time now. How are you both?"

Imbolondo, Chief Ikabonga's great black bull is standing on the river bank looking at us. Mokoro pushes his pole into the mud at the bottom of the river and brings the canoe to a halt.

"Greetings, good Mokoro," Imbolondo says to him. "I have a warning for you and the children. Come closer to the shore and I will give you the news."

Imbolondo walks into the river, puts his nose into the water and snorts bubbles into it. He lifts his head, shakes it and blows water all over the three of us while he considers what he is going to tell us.

"I had just arrived back here after taking you to the edge of the Evergreen Forest." Imbolondo says. "when a motorboat came up the river to visit Chief Ikabonga. It was a boat with an engine that screamed loudly. It was a boat that was as bright and shiny as the sun and it travelled at a great speed over the backs of hippos and crocodiles. It is the nature of powerful men to use these boats to impress fishermen like Chief Ikabonga. It is the nature of Chief Ikabonga to like rich men who flatter him with beer and money."

"Do you know who this man is?" Chibwe asks Imbolondo.

"No, I don't know his name, but you and Chipo do know him," Imbolondo replies and he stops to graze for a while.

My stomach isn't dancing any more. It's jumping around in fright.

"My advice to you two children," Imbolondo says, "is not to stop at Chief Ikabonga's village tonight. He has promised to keep you prisoners in his village while he sends a message to the Small Town. There are people there who also like money and rich men. They will capture you and send you back to the Big City to this powerful man."

"How did he know we had been here before?" I ask in disbelief.

"How did he find out that we were on our way to the Evergreen Forest?" Chibwe asks Imbolondo. "Who told him?"

"Your Aunt Chimunya thought this powerful man had kidnapped you once again. She sent the police to his office. That's how he found out where you were going. He frightened your Aunt and made her tell him everything about your plans to go to the Evergreen Forest. He spoke of this with laughter to a sunburnt, red-faced man with yellow hair who came with him in the boat."

Imbolondo's belly rumbles loudly and he drops a heap of dung on the grass behind him.

"My advice to you, Mokoro, is to avoid this rich man and his speeding boat," Imbolondo says and he nudges Mokoro's pole with the tip of one of his great horns. "This rich man will sink your dugout canoe to the bottom of the Great River with you tied underneath it."

I can't speak a word because I've forgotten how to breathe.

Mokoro says nothing but his head goes up and down and his eyes blink very fast.

"Thank you, Imbolondo," Chibwe says. "You are a good friend to us and you've saved our lives again."

"It's in my nature to behave as I do." Imbolondo says. "It's in the nature of Mokoro to always finish what he has promised to do. He will take care of you both. Go well my three friends. Be brave and keep safe."

Imbolondo bellows softly and then canters away to join the rest of his herd of cattle on the hill behind him.

Mokoro signs to us to lie down low in the dugout canoe. He points at the sun and we understand that we must wait for darkness to fall. Then he pushes the dugout canoe back and back in among some tall thick reeds until we are completely hidden and all that can be seen is a tiny bit of the top of Mokoro's pole.

We wait for the night.

CHAPTER TWO
THE GREAT RIVER

We wait for a long time after the sun has set. Mokoro stands as usual on one leg, balanced by his pole. He doesn't speak. He listens. From where we are hiding, we can hear the sounds of voices and laughter from Chief Ikabonga's village. Chibwe and I have both learnt that sounds carry clearly for long distances over water. Even on a night as dark as tonight, fishermen would soon notice a sound that wasn't made by a fish or a hippo. We wait until we can't see a spark from the village fire and there are no more sounds from humans. At last, Mokoro slides the dugout canoe out of the reeds and we move without a splash down the river until we can't smell the smoke of their dying fire any more. Neither Chibwe or I dare whisper and I feel swollen to bursting with questions and mosquito bites. After a long time, Mokoro stops the canoe, raises his hand to test the wind and smiles at us with a finger on his lips. The wind is blowing towards us from the village so we can talk quietly.

"How will Mokoro find his way down the river in the dark?"

"Do you think Aunt Chimunya is safe?"

"Do you think Wally and Winnie posted our letter to her?"

"Will we only be able to travel in the dark from now on?"

"Will we get lost?"

"How far away is the Small Town?"

"When will we get past the Small Town safely?"

"Will the mosquitoes ever stop biting?"

"How far do we still have to go?"

"If Mokoro could speak would he be able to answer our questions?"

"Do you think we'll ever have answers to our questions?"

We turn to Mokoro and look up at him. He smiles at us but, as usual, he says nothing. He continues to pole us on down the river while overhead millions of stars are slowly spinning us towards the day and under the dugout canoe the Great River ripples and swirls. Its waters flow on as black as the night, except when creatures or fish break the surface and it sparkles with life.

As the sun is rising, Mokoro pushes the canoe up against a sandy, reed-covered island and we all step out onto flat earth and stretch. I light a small driftwood fire and Chibwe and Mokoro catch some fish for our breakfast.

"Mokoro, what are your plans?" I ask him. "I know you can't speak, but perhaps you can show us where you are going to take us."

Mokoro shakes his head from side to side.

"As we know Mokoro shakes his head when he means to say 'Yes!'" Chibwe reminds me.

"Where is the Small Town?" Chibwe asks and Mokoro points east to the rising sun.

"Where are you taking us Mokoro?" I ask him and Mokoro points southwards and then makes a big circle with his arm.

"Is that a safe way for us to travel?" Chibwe asks, and Mokoro shakes his head, nods and laughs and throws his hands out sideways.

"I don't think he really knows," Chibwe says to me. "But neither do we or anyone else!"

"I feel safe with you, Mokoro," I say.

"Thank you for looking after us, Mokoro," Chibwe says and we smile.

"Let's eat," Chibwe says and we do, all three of us. We're all hungry after our long night in the canoe and all the waiting we had to do before we set out.

***

We travel on the river at night and hide away on islands in the flood plains during the day. Mokoro seems to be able to sense his way in the dark and we never seem to bump into hippos or crocodiles by accident. I begin to wonder if Mokoro has some knowledge that most people don't until I remember that Mokoro also knows Mama Wati and she is a friend of all the river creatures. Chibwe and I have time to talk to each other when Mokoro goes fishing.

"Why do you think Mr Wabenzi keeps on chasing us?" I ask Chibwe. "It can't be because we escaped from Ma Richwoman. We're only children and there are plenty of other street kids for him to take prisoner and sell."

"That's true," Chibwe answers. "I don't think it's because of what we saw in the Pa Badman's store, either. Who would believe us if Mr Wabenzi says that we're lying? We're only children."

"Do you suppose," I say, after I've thought about it for a while. "Do you suppose that Mr Wabenzi doesn't want us to stop Kambili's witchcraft and end the drought?"

"It's hard to believe that any sensible person would want the drought to carry on," Chibwe answers. "The drought harms the land and hurts people. It's wrong to want that to happen."

"It must be because of the copper mine that he wants to make in the Valley. He was talking about mining for copper on the television at Aunt Chimunya's house," I say. "He says the drought makes people leave the Valley and it's easier for him to get permission to mine for copper if nobody lives there."

"I suppose there must be a few people who will hurt other people and other creatures in order to get very rich," Chibwe says, frowning.

"It must mean that our journey to find Makemba so we can end Kambili's drought is very important," I say.

Chibwe and I look at each other and shake our heads as Mokoro does.

"We're only children!" we say together.

"I'm afraid!" I say. "I want to go home to Ma and Pa!"

"Me too!" Chibwe agrees. "But all we can do is carry on!"

"How can what we're doing be so important?" I ask.

"Mr Wabenzi thinks it is — he wants to stop us," Chibwe says.

An even more frightening idea comes to me.

"Perhaps Kambili is making Mr Wabenzi chase us!

Perhaps Mr Wabenzi is doing what Kambili wants him to do!

We know Kambili wanted to kill us!

Has Kambili become so powerful that Mr Wabenzi obeys her?

Are Ma and Pa still alive?"

CHAPTER THREE
THE DEEP CHASM

Some of our nights on the river with Mokoro pass like a dream. There comes a time when we stop travelling at night and go back to travelling during the daytime. We are still careful to avoid villages and places where people are camping or canoeing on the river but Mokoro seems to be able to tell when he can trust people. He watches to see how they behave with each other and most of all he watches them to see how they treat the river and the wilderness around them. Once or twice we are invited to share food with villagers or fishermen. Once we spend an evening with a solitary birdwatcher who is almost as tongue-tied as Mokoro is silent.

After a while the waters leave the flood plain and begin to collect all their differing streams together into a deeper, wider and swifter river. Mokoro lays his pole down in the canoe and picks up a long paddle that he uses as a rudder to steer us into quieter waters when the river is flowing fast and he doesn't want to lose control. Soon after that we see ahead of us a towering wall of cloud or smoke that rises up into the hot blue sky and seems to completely block our way down the river.

"What is that?" Chibwe asks, astonished.

"It can't be a fire," I say. "Fires race across the countryside and this stays always in the same place."

We can hear Mokoro laughing behind us. His smile is the widest we have ever seen. Every one of his pointed sharp teeth glitters in his face.

Crowding in from the river banks on either side of the wall of smoke we can see green rainforest.

"The rainforest isn't burning!" Chibwe says. "It's not smoke from a fire – it's spray from the river!"

"What's that noise? It sounds like thunder!" I say, staring ahead. "What is happening to the river?"

"It's a waterfall!" Chibwe shouts. "The river is falling over a cliff."

We turn in horror to Mokoro for help.

Mokoro is flinging his fishing net out over the water in front of the canoe and the strangest, harshest cries come from his throat. It's the begging sound of baby pelicans. In answer to his calls, we see a huge flock of the great white birds flying down the river towards us. The canoe has only just floated over the spread-out fishing net when a hundred pelicans swoop down and gather up the outer edges of it in their enormous beaks. We are suspended inside a fishing net hammock up high in the air. We are flying through the spray and thunder made by the Great River as it plunges into a deep narrow chasm.

We can say nothing at all. Our mouths are wide open in shock.

Behind us, Mokoro is laughing aloud with pleasure.

All around us are perfect circular hoops of rainbows as we are carried through clouds of misty water spray. We are soaked with river water that rises up with the force of the falling river and then falls back down like rain. We're deafened by the roar of the waterfall and we're stunned by the power of the river. Far too soon, we are past the Deep Chasm into which the

Great River is disappearing and we are soaring towards a new wilderness of zigzagging canyons and rapids that race away from the water fall. We are flying higher even than the eagles that hunt over the river.

We will never be able to forget what we have seen.

We will never be able to forget our flight over the magnificent Great River Falls.

***

The pelicans carry the fishing net with the canoe and the three of us suspended in it for a long way. The river gorge below us is narrow and the river descends for miles through fearsome rapids. We keep very still so that we don't upset the balance of the canoe. Mokoro looks for the first time as if he is asleep, spread-eagled in the canoe.

"The river seems to be turning north-east again," Chibwe says quietly to me.

"Home is north-east isn't it?" I ask. "Mokoro signed that the river would take us in a wide curve around the Big City."

"This way we should be safe from Mr Wabenzi at least." Chibwe looks satisfied.

"It's wonderful to be flying with the pelicans isn't it!" I say. "It's also terrifying!"

"They're so beautiful in the air."

"They were so smelly and clumsy on the lagoon where we first saw them."

"Look what's ahead of us, Chipo!" Chibwe says. "It's an enormous lake!"

The setting sun is behind us and the sky has turned red.

In front of us pale pink water stretches out as smooth as glass among dark hills. The pelicans begin to descend towards it in slanting circles that slowly get lower and lower. Mokoro wakes and makes his strange throaty noises again. I don't want our flight to come to an end but I know that I do want to have my feet on solid ground again or at least to be swimming in the water which will be better at holding me up than the air and wind around us now.

Our landing is so sudden that Chibwe and I are both breathless. Around us the pelicans hit the water one by one with much splashing and paddling. The canoe dips forwards, then recovers without taking in much water but Mokoro, Chibwe and I have all felt the coolness of the lake water on our skins and know it will soon be dark. The pelicans have begun to skim the water for food and gather together in circles.

Mokoro finishes his strange conversation with them and turns to us with his wide smile.

"Mokoro, that was magic," we say to him. "How do we thank the pelicans for their help? Please tell them we're very grateful."

Mokoro starts to pull in his fishing net. In those few moments it has already filled with shining, flapping fish. Mokoro, Chibwe and I throw the fish into the pelicans' beaks until, satisfied, they swim away. We keep just enough for our own supper and Mokoro begins to paddle the canoe towards the rocky shore of the hills around the lake.

CHAPTER FOUR
THE OLD PEOPLE

Now that we are on the surface of the Wide Lake, Chibwe and I can see that it goes on for many miles. From the steep hills around it we know it must be very deep.

"This lake is immense," Chibwe says. "We saw how far it stretches when we were flying up high with the pelicans but now, we know it's enormous, even though we can only see part of it."

"It will take us years and years to paddle all the way to the other end," I say. "It makes me feel so small and weak."

Chibwe gives me a strange look. The canoe has stopped moving forwards.

"Mokoro, can I help you and paddle the canoe?" he asks.

Mokoro hands the paddle over to Chibwe. We are shocked to see that he is crying. His face looks sad and crumpled and tears are running down his cheeks. He points towards the shore and waves with his hand at a solitary grass hut on the shore. We know we must go over there. Mokoro curls up in the bottom of the boat and we hear him sobbing and groaning.

"What's wrong Mokoro? Was the journey too hard for you? What can we do?" I ask him. I keep patting his shoulder but he doesn't stop crying.

"I think someone he loves has died.

"I say. "Grandmother was like this when Grandfather died."

Chibwe paddles us to the shore. We both jump out and pull

the canoe up onto a sandy beach. Mokoro stays on the boat by himself. We can't move him and his crying sounds louder and sadder. When we turn to face the hut, we see a thin old man and a tiny old woman watching us. I thought they were two very old tree trunks with cracked bark and covered on top with white moss, until they spoke.

"You have come at last! Welcome, Chibwe and Chipo," the thin old man says.

"The Ghosts of the Lake are haunting Mokoro," the tiny old woman says. "He is grieving for our Ancestors buried under the waters."

"The two of you must make the offerings to the Ancestors so that Mokoro can be free."

"How do we do that?" I ask them. "What do we do?"

"Why are his Ancestors buried under the Lake?" Chibwe asks.

"First of all," the tiny woman says, "we must eat the supper of fish that you have brought us and then we will tell you the story of the Wide Lake and the Drowned Ancestors."

"What about Mokoro?" I say.

"Did you not see that Mama Wati is singing to him," the old man says.

Chibwe and I look back at the canoe and we see that Mama Wati is in the water by the canoe and she is stroking Mokoro's head.

"Shusha-shusha-shusha-slapa-shusha-sleepa," she sings.

The song sounds like water lapping on the beach and we are happy to see that Mokoro is asleep and no longer crying.

"When we were children, the same age as you are now," the old man begins his story, "there was no lake here. The Great River ran through these hills and the God of the River, the powerful River God Snake, lived in its waters and brought both floods and food to these valleys every year from the Faraway Lands."

"When we were children, the same age as you are now," the old woman says, "strangers came to the land. They had no understanding of the Great River and its peoples. They built a strong wall and trapped the Great River and the River God,"

"When we were children, the same age as you are now," the old man continues, "we lived in a valley by the shores of the Great River. In that valley we buried our Ancestors and every year we came to see them and give them offerings of food and beer so that they would remember us with kindness."

"After the Great River and the River God were trapped by the wall the strangers built, our homes and the graves of our Ancestors were drowned by deep waters," the old woman says. "Every year at that same time, the Ghosts of the Ancestors come to haunt their lost children. Mokoro is one of those who suffers from the hauntings of the Ghosts and so are we."

"Tomorrow, Chibwe and Chipo, you must take the offerings of food and beer to the place above the graves of the Ancestors so that they stop haunting Mokoro," the old man says. "If you don't, Mokoro must stay here and weep forever and you won't be able to carry on with your journey."

"How do we know where to go or what to do?" Chibwe asks the two old people.

"Your sister knows the answers," the old woman replies. "The Spirits will speak to your sister."

"We need a more powerful boat," I say with a frown because I don't want to listen to the Spirits again. "The Wide Lake is big and we don't have the strength of the River God."

"We will see what Mama Wati brings us in the morning," the old man says.

***

In the early morning we go down to the river bank to find that the canoe has vanished. In its place is a bigger, green banana-shaped boat with a motor-engine on its stern. Mokoro sits inside it with tears running down his face and his head in his hands. The bag of seeds, Makemba's water bottle and the fishing nets are all in there too. Chibwe kicks the side of the boat to see if it is our dugout canoe covered with paint but it's made of something lighter than wood. The old man shows Chibwe and me how to start the engine and how to steer the boat. He points out two spare fuel tanks and demonstrates how to refill the engine fuel tank.

"You should reach the Ancestors' Graves on one fuel tank, Chibwe," the old man says. "After that you will have to plan where you can go to get more fuel. If Mokoro recovers from his hauntings, he will know the places to get fuel. If there is a storm you must find a safe harbour on the lee of an island."

"Keep going straight up the middle of the lake towards that dip between those two hills. When the sun is over your heads you will be close to the Ancestors' Graves and there you must make the offering of food and beer."

"Chipo and Mokoro, you will know when you have reached the right place. Hold hands when you are there so that the Spirits can talk to both of you," the old woman says. "Go well children. Go well Mokoro, old friend."

The two old people push the boat out while Chibwe starts the engine. They watch and wave until we can't see them any more. All I can think about is what the Spirits of the Ancestors will want me to do this time.

CHAPTER FIVE
SPIRITS OF THE ANCESTORS

Chibwe steers the boat steadily towards the dip in the hills. The lake is smooth and quiet but the water glitters in the already hot sun. The only other boat we see is a large ferry full of tourists and cars travelling back the other way. They don't notice us because we're too small. We have to concentrate on the way we're going because the hills around the lake are confusing and if we get too close to the shore, we find ourselves among dead trees that are as hard as iron and that could make holes in our banana-shaped boat. We made an early start this morning and we travel for several hours before the sun is overhead. When I think it almost is time, I take hold of Mokoro's hand and shut my eyes. I don't know what to expect or when it will happen. Then Mokoro screams in pain and I feel a jolt of energy go right through my body.

"It's here!" I shout. I know my voice sounds like a frog croaking, but I don't care. I feel myself fly through the air. Mokoro lets go of my hand but something or someone much stronger has my other hand and is pulling me into the lake. I'm diving into deep green water so far down that I can't see or breathe. I'm drowning and all around me are the Ghosts of the Ancestors and all people who lived in the valley before the waters covered them.

"Don't forget us!" they scream.

"Don't leave us!" they cry.

"If you forget us then you will also die!"

"If you leave us then you will also be forgotten!"

"Do not forget your roots!" they call.

"Do not forget your Ancestors!"

"Do not forget the River!"

"Do not forget the trees!"

"Do not forget us!"

"Do not forget those who fought and died to live by the river."

I see that Mama Wati is swimming with me. She's holding my hand and somehow, I can breathe under the water just as she can.

I can also speak.

"We'll never forget you!" I call.

"We'll always remember you!" I promise.

"We belong together!" I say.

I'm also able to see even down here in the dark deep waters. I can see all the Ghosts, the fighters with spears, the Chiefs, the wise sanganas, the men, and the women and children. All the Ancestors are here with me and speaking to me. I see the stones that mark their graves on the bottom of the lake.

A monstrous whirlpool is surging around me, it goes faster and faster, and gets bigger and bigger until I think I'm in the centre of all the water that poured down the Great River into the Deep Chasm. It thunders and it roars and I know that I'm seeing a small part of the enormous God of the River. The force of his power is crushing me but I'm spinning faster and faster and rising and rising until I'm thrown back into the boat soaking wet and gasping. Mama Wati has let go of my hand.

"It's here!" I say. "This is the place to make the offerings. Mokoro – you must give the Ancestors the food and the beer we have brought for them, now!"

Mokoro leaps to his feet tipping the boat dangerously.

He takes the pot of maize meal and tips it into the swirling sucking hole in the water beside the boat. We watch it disappear into the hungry funnelling waters. He grabs the pot of beer and holds it up over his head. Before he pours it into the water, he takes a long drink himself. Chibwe reaches up anxiously but Mokoro shouts aloud and the rest of the beer joins the maize meal in the lake. For a moment I think the boat will also be sucked down the whirlpool as it rocks around on the circling waves.

The lake becomes calm again.

Mokoro is making chanting sounds at the top of his voice without using any words. He's drumming on the empty beer and maize pots. Chibwe and I join in and clap our hands and we sing the words we know.

"Celebrate the Ancestors!

"The Ancestors are good!

"The Ancestors are our roots!

"The Ancestors are the source of our life!

"The Ancestors are the river of our lives!"

Mokoro stops drumming and chanting and falls asleep on the fishing nets. He snores loudly.

Chibwe starts the engine again and we carry on down the lake towards the dam wall.

CHAPTER SIX
THE WIND STORM ON THE WIDE LAKE

Next morning Mokoro takes over steering the boat again. He still doesn't speak but he does whistle sometimes and he smiles again. We are travelling much faster now. The noisy engine on our boat churns up the water behind us and leaves a long white trail of foam that someone might be able to follow. Mokoro signs that the next time the sun sets we will have reached the other end of the lake. Chibwe and I have to shout at each other over the engine noise when we want to talk.

"It feels like the school holidays," I shout at Chibwe. He laughs.

"I feel like I'm on holiday because we're so far from Mr Wabenzi. This lake is so wide and there are so few other boats on it."

"We know now that there's a big dam wall blocking the Great River," I say. "How will we get over that? Will we fly again? Will we walk around it? We'll need to have a canoe if we're going to travel down the river, won't we?"

Neither of us is worried.

"We survived so far. It must get better," Chibwe says.

We're still laughing later in the afternoon when Mokoro slows the boat down. He lifts one fuel tank. It's empty. The other is light. It's half full. He taps the engine and points towards the shore where there's a scruffy store and a rickety landing stage. Mokoro doesn't seem worried.

"We need to buy more fuel I think," Chibwe says.

"How do we pay?" I ask.

"I don't know," Chibwe says. "Fish, maybe?"

That's when we see the big white motor launch anchored just off the shore. There are some women in bikinis sitting under an awning on the roof with wine glasses in front of them. A couple of men are fishing off the side and another person is cooking meat on a barbecue on the deck. Chibwe and I sit up and stare.

"Those people must be very rich," I say. "I've never seen a boat that big before."

"That motor launch must cost even more than Mr Wabenzi's limousine. Why is it here?" Chibwe says. We look at each other and suddenly, I feel sick.

"Look!" I hiss at Chibwe. "There's that fat man with the red face and the yellow hair that was on the television with Mr Wabenzi. That's Mr Willy Waffell!"

Willy Waffell is leaning on the boat rail with a self-satisfied expression on his face. He wears golden swimming trunks and his body is bright red above and sweaty white below his overhanging belly.

Mokoro is watching the motor launch too as we chug past slowly. His flapping hand tells us to lie down in the boat so we can't be seen. He taps the fuel tank again. We do have to get more fuel. We have to hope that nobody will connect Mokoro with the two children and the bag of seeds and water that Mr Wabenzi has been hunting. No one could forget Mokoro once they've seen him. His smile and his silence are unique.

"We haven't seen Mr Wabenzi yet," Chibwe says. "Maybe he isn't on the boat."

"We'll have to find out what we can by ourselves," I say. "Mokoro can't ask questions. He can only listen."

We climb out of the banana boat and hang around with the children on the shore who are giggling at the behaviour of the people on the motor launch. They repeat aloud the rumours that their parents only whisper to each other and they laugh about them.

"Wabenzi owns that boat."

"Wabenzi uses his boat to smuggle money across the border."

"Wabenzi leaves his wives at home."

"Wabenzi brings many girlfriends on the boat."

"Wabenzi's friend is sooooo rich!"

"Wabenzi's friend has a funny voice."

The children imitate Wabenzi's friend.

"What waffely wonderfully cute kiddies you are. We will waffell theeth kiddies thome cute shiny coins won't we! Yeth! Your daddies and mummies like uth! Yeth!"

I know they mean Willy Waffell.

One of the older boys doesn't laugh at Mr Wabenzi. He spits in the direction of the motor launch.

"Wabenzi uses bad magic to make droughts. He is a friend of Kambili, the Drought Witch. He wants the drought to get rid of the farmers and the animals," the boy says. "When people are poor, they go to dig precious stones for him. Sometimes poor people kill elephants for him. He doesn't care if poor people die."

"How do you know that?" Chibwe asks him.

"My father went to work for him in the Valley. He came home once and he told my mother and me about Wabenzi and Kambili. After that, we never saw my father again."

"You must be sad," I say and the boy nods. There are tears in his eyes.

"Why is Wabenzi here?" Chibwe asks. "This is not a place that rich people come to visit."

"He has spies here," the boy says. "They are watching in case someone comes this way from the Evergreen Forest with good magic to end the drought."

I have to swallow my fear twice before I ask him, "What will this someone with good magic look like?"

"Wabenzi says they are children but I don't think they can be ordinary children, do you?"

"No!" I say. "Powerful children would have to be tall and strong and beautiful. I don't suppose they are ever afraid, either."

Chibwe tugs my arm. Mokoro is looking for us. We run to the banana boat. A man in a baseball cap is standing by it and looking at our bag of seeds.

"Is this for medicine for Spirits?" he asks.

"Our mother makes necklaces with those seeds," Chibwe says.

We push the boat out and Mokoro starts the engine.

The man watches us for a few minutes. I see him turn in the direction of the motor launch and raise his hand to wave at those on board.

"Mama Wati! Mama Wati!" I call. "We need your help please."

That's when the wind starts to blow.

***

When the wind blows on a land-locked lake it raises high steep waves that are very close together. We soon feel as if the banana boat will be battered until it is broken into bits by the impact of so many waves. Every wave we hit splashes over the prow and sloshes some water into the boat. There are no clouds or rain, only this fierce strong wind blowing towards the south-west. The sun is hot but we're wet, bruised and helpless. I clutch onto the side of the boat and manage to look back over my shoulder. Mr Wabenzi's motor launch is catching up on us. It's also slamming hard into every single wave. Its passengers must be uncomfortable too but that doesn't reassure those of us in the banana boat. They aren't in any danger of overturning and we are.

"They're going to run us down and sink our boat!" Chibwe shouts.

"We must save Makemba's seeds and the water from the Source of the Great River," I shout back.

Mokoro is fighting to keep the boat straight into the wind but the engine is starting to fail.

I concentrate all my thoughts on one hope and I call out again.

"Mama Wati!"

I see what I think is a huge black fish beside us in the water or maybe an overturned boat that has bobbed up next to us.

Perhaps we've turned sideways to the wind and are going over ourselves. In the next moment I realise it is a giant woman with two fish tails. Mama Wati is reaching out for each of us. She swoops all our belongings into Mokoro's fishing net and gathers the three of us into her arms. With two flicks of her tail she sends the banana boat into a spinning flop in front of Wabenzi's boat. I hear a cry from the deck and see someone point at it.

"They'll believe we are all drowned!" I think.

After that I wonder if we are, in fact, all drowned and dead. Mama Wati's two tails send us racing through the waves while she cuddles us in her arms as if we are babies. Sometimes we are under and sometimes over the water, sometimes gasping, and sometimes breathing air. Sometimes I think I'm dreaming that I'm a fish and I live my entire life in water.

CHAPTER SEVEN
THE JOURNEY

I don't remember if, or when, the sun set yesterday, but it's morning now and the sun is high when I wake. Mokoro is cooking us some fish for breakfast and there are bananas waiting to be eaten by the fire. Chibwe is yawning and stretching. The bag of seeds and the bottle of water sit next to Mokoro's fishing net. We are camping by a dirt track on a bank above the lake. The water is still rough but there's only a light breeze today.

"Good morning," I say. "Where are we? Where's Mama Wati?"

Mokoro's hand points first to the dam wall, next the river below it, and last a wave of farewell to Mama Wati. He smiles and points at our food.

"What do we do now?" Chibwe asks.

Eat first, then wait, then something will come, say Mokoro's hands, so that's what we do.

"What happened yesterday?" I ask. "Did Mama Wati really save us all or were we just washed up here after the boat sank?"

"Chipo – you know what happened!" Chibwe says.

"I do know. I don't know if I believe what I know," I say.

As soon as we've eaten and stamped out the camp fire we hear the sound of an engine. I want to run and hide but Mokoro smiles. His hand taps his chest near his heart to say it is his friend who is approaching.

A battered pickup truck rattles up and shudders to a halt and an old, grey lady with round yellow eyes shakes her way out of the driver's seat and stands up with the help of a stick. At first, I think that it's the old pickup that has made her tremble but when she doesn't stop twitching, I wonder if she's the reason the pickup bumped around so much.

"Oooh! Did you know," she says and her voice goes up and down. "Yesterday during that big wind storm on the lake, Mr Wabenzi's motor launch had engine failure and was blown onto a rocky island and damaged. Nobody was hurt but they were all afraid and miserable and had to spend the night there waiting to be rescued.

"They do say that two children and a man in a banana boat were drowned. Their boat was washed ashore close by Mr Wabenzi's boat. Fancy that"!

The old grey lady gives us a big slow wink.

"We must be quick," she says. "Mokoro needs to be close to a river or water all the time. Car journeys aren't good for him."

Chibwe and I climb into the back of the pickup with our seeds, water and fishing net. Mokoro and the old grey lady sit in the cab and speak to each other by holding hands.

"Who is she?" I whisper to Chibwe. "How did she know that we needed a lift?"

"Mokoro must have sent her a message. Last night I heard him hooting like an owl," Chibwe says.

I shake my head. There's so much I don't understand.

The old grey lady starts the pickup and drives us down secret tracks, across roads when there's no traffic, over hills until we find ourselves down in the river gorge below the dam wall. The Great River is free again and flowing swiftly between high rocky cliffs covered in dense forest. Waiting for us on a narrow stony ledge by the river, is Mokoro's dugout canoe and his pole and his paddle. Mokoro tumbles out of the pickup and falls over. He waves at the Great River and opens his mouth. Chibwe and I run to fetch him a drink of river water and soon he is his old strong self again.

"I didn't know that Mokoro cannot leave the river," Chibwe says.

"Neither did I" I say. "I'm glad that he is still with us now! I don't think we could manage without him."

Only with Mokoro's help can we hope to complete the last part of our long journey home.

The grey old lady flutters down to say goodbye to Mokoro. She blinks her eyes at us when we thank her and waves us away.

"GOOOoooo weeEEEL!" she calls as the Great River carries the canoe with all three of us swiftly away down the gorge.

***

After the Wide Lake and the Big Storm, the Narrow Gorge feels like a private and peaceful kingdom that belongs only to wild animals. There are solitary leopards, troops of baboons, rock hyrax, snakes, crocodiles and all kinds of eagles and owls and herons that eat fish. Mokoro steers us through the gorge but doesn't have to paddle or use his pole to push us on because the river flows fast and free.

We leave the beauty of the gorge much too soon and find ourselves among sand white dunes that have been spilt over the valley by the waters of the Great River. Further on we are surrounded by banana groves and we see many farmers and fishermen. We come to a place where all the trees have been cut down and all that is left is bare pink earth. No food grows on it and the people who live there are thin and tired and sit down all day. It's a new desert. I know that it will make Makemba cry when she sees it.

We wait for midnight to paddle secretly under a high long bridge that carries hundreds of lorries and cars to the neighbouring country during the day. Mokoro is suspicious of the people who work here and we know we must be careful not to be seen by any of Mr Wabenzi's spies.

Several days later we arrive in another wilderness. Mokoro paddles us past pods of hippo, herds of elephants, zebras, puku and wildebeest. The river is full of fish and there are birds everywhere. At night we camp under winterthorn or waterberry trees. Sometimes we sleep on rocky islands, sometimes we spend the night on sandy beaches. As he has always done, Mokoro stands first on one leg, then on the other. He watches first with one eye, then with the other until the sun rises. He seems to never need to sleep.

CHAPTER EIGHT
DOUBTS AND DIFFICULTIES

The Great River is beautiful. There are so many wonderful and unusual plants, insects, birds, animals and fish that Chibwe and I are always happy and always making new and wonderful discoveries about the world that we live in.

"I want to live here forever," I say to Chibwe. "I want Pa and Ma to come and live with us on the banks of the Great River. We would always be happy here."

"We can't stay here," Chibwe says. "We don't know what's happening to Pa and Ma. We don't even know if they are still alive. We don't know if they're still prisoners of Kambili. How do we get hold of them and bring them here? Kambili won't let us do that!"

"I don't want to go back!" I say. "I'm afraid of Kambili. I'm afraid of Wabenzi. I don't think we can rescue Ma and Pa. I don't think we can stop the drought! It's too hard for us. It's too much work. We haven't even begun to plant the seeds yet."

Chibwe doesn't say anything for a while. He looks at me and he chews his bottom lip. Then he looks at Mokoro.

"Perhaps Mokoro will look after you. Perhaps the two of you can stay here where it's safe. I can go on by myself. I'll plant the seeds. It'll take me a bit longer but I think I can do it. You've been ever so brave Chipo. You deserve to have a rest."

Chibwe is being kind and grown-up. It makes me so cross.

"You can't go by yourself, Chibwe! You needed me all the

way. I think we should just give up! Now! We should stop! We should stay here!"

Chibwe is upset.

"I know you don't want to carry on, either!" I shout.

Chibwe is silent. Mokoro sits down and puts his head in his hands. I look at them both and I start to cry loudly.

"I hate you Chibwe! I hate you Mokoro! I want to go home! I want this place to be my home!"

We're all sitting on a beach by the river after our supper of fish and fruit. There's a steep bank behind us and above that a forest of trees.

I turn and I run away from Chibwe and Mokoro until I find a gap in the bank where I can climb up and vanish among the trees.

When I get onto the top of the bank I stop.

I want to cry myself to sleep but I know I can't do that. I wouldn't be safe alone, here in the wilderness. I kick the ground and a lizard runs away. I throw a stone into the trees and some birds fly out. Some creature is moving in the trees. I'm too upset to be sensible and I can't make the right decisions when I'm afraid. I go back to the edge of the bank and sit down and look at the river.

"Talk to me Great River," I ask. "Please, tell me what I must do."

I remember what Makemba said to me at the Source of the Great River in the Evergreen Forest.

"Chipo! Can you cry enough tears to end the drought?

Think of your brother! Perhaps he needs your help?

A river that forgets its source will dry up.

A people that forget their roots will not be able to survive."

I'm looking down on the Great River below me. I can hear the sounds it makes as it flows past. It is talking to me. It tells me that it doesn't stop doing what a river does. It carries on flowing down to the sea. No river can run backwards. No life can be lived backwards.

When I travelled with the Rain Spirits, they took me all over the world, so I've seen the sea. I've seen that water is life. I've seen that the river is always the same and always changing. The river that Chibwe, Mokoro and I travelled on has left us and gone on ahead of us to the sea. The river that runs past me now is a different river that knows different people. I'm only one tiny part of the River that is Life. All I can do is be that tiny living part of the River of Life. No matter how much I cry, that is all that I am.

The Great River has spoken to me. I know what I must do.

I slip and slide down the bank and walk back to the camp fire and my brother, Chibwe and my friend, Mokoro.

"I'm sorry Chibwe," I say. "I'm sorry Mokoro. Forgive me. Tomorrow we've got work to do. We have to go and rescue Ma and Pa. We have to go back home and defeat Kambili, the Drought Witch. I'm coming with you."

Chibwe and I hug each other and Mokoro smiles and pats us on our heads.

***

There are some things that Chibwe and I don't like to talk about. We never talk about how much school we've missed or what we'll do when we grow up. The journey has made us both strong and fit but we're rather thin. I've grown a little taller but Chibwe is much taller and his clothes don't fit him very well. Mokoro's shorts have always been ragged but he hasn't changed as much as we have. We don't have a mirror, so while we know what the other looks like, we have no idea what we, ourselves, look like. My hair has got much longer and I tie it up with a strip of cloth, but Mokoro had to use Palma's penknife to cut Chibwe's hair when it got in his eyes. I laughed when I saw how he looked. That was mean of me.

"I'm going to be rich like Wabenzi when I grow up," Chibwe says one day.

"Why?" I say. "Wabenzi's horrid. Why do you want to be like him?"

"I don't want to be like him, you stupid girl!" Chibwe snaps back at me. "If I was rich, I would do good things with my money."

I don't answer at once. I need to think.

"What would you do with your money?" I ask after a while.

"Buy a tractor for Pa. Buy a television for us! Pay for us to go to university."

"What would you buy for Ma?"

"I don't know" Chibwe says after a bit. "Ma is happy. She doesn't want anything much."

"Do you think money can get rid of Kambili? Or stop Wabenzi's mine? Or end the drought?"

"I don't know," Chibwe says. "I wish I did but maybe that's what we need to do."

Dust and Rain

Something is making Chibwe restless. Perhaps he misses his school friends. Perhaps he wants a girlfriend. Perhaps younger sisters and silent fishermen aren't such good company.

***

Mokoro brings the canoe to a stop earlier than usual today. We've been travelling through a second, high gorge where once again the Great River runs swiftly. He hasn't had to work so hard to get here but he seems worried by the next stage of our journey. I have a feeling that things are going to change again.

Mokoro's hands explain that we're near the end of this second gorge and very soon the Great River will be joined by another river. This is the Sandy River that we must travel up to go back home to our farm. It will be very hard work, his hands say, because the river will be flowing towards him and he will have to paddle against the current. The weather will be much hotter too he says pointing at the sun above us and he rubs his hand across his forehead to wipe tomorrow's sweat away.

In the evening we are joined at our meal by a strange wandering man. He didn't come on a canoe and he didn't walk here because there are no paths down the gorge. He sits on his heels by our fire with his knees folded up. His arms are long and his elbows stick out sideways. He keeps his head on one side. He reminds me of a cormorant drying its wings. He seems to be a friend of Mokoro's but we never find out his name.

"The drought in the Valley keeps getting worse," he says. "Mr Wabenzi often comes to the Valley to see a very important person called Kambili – a very big, fat, important person called Kambili.

"She lives on the farm that once belonged to Pa Mulenga and Ma Chiluba and their two children."

"The children have vanished and nobody has seen Pa Mulenga or Ma Chiluba for a very long time."

CHAPTER NINE
SEEDS AND WATER

We leave the Great River and Mokoro turns his dugout canoe onto the Sandy River that runs all the way home past our farm and into the Eastern hills. By this time, we all have a sense that things are not going very well. Mokoro poles us up the river all day but there are a couple of stretches where Chibwe and I have to get out to make the canoe lighter and we walk beside it through shallow waters. Once, we have to pull the canoe off a sandbank. That's when Chibwe stops.

"It's no good, Mokoro," he says. "No amount of effort and willpower on your part will get this canoe all the way to our home. It's time for us to thank you and say goodbye."

"You need to be on water or beside water, Mokoro," I say. "The Sandy River is drying up. We have to go on without you."

"We'll never be able to thank you enough or repay what you have done for us," Chibwe says.

Mokoro shakes his head from side to side. He looks as sad as we feel.

His hands say go on, go well, destroy the Drought Witch, bring back the rains and that will be enough.

"We'll do our best," Chibwe says.

"We'll do what we can!" I say.

We both hug Mokoro and the three of us cry but we all know that even our tears must not be wasted. We unpack all the things we need from Mokoro's canoe, the seeds, the water, and the fishing net bags to carry them in and we have our last meal and spend our last night together.

In the morning we push Mokoro off in his canoe. It goes much faster with the river's sluggish current than against it and Mokoro and the canoe soon vanish from our sight. Chibwe and I turn to walk up the river together. We can use it like a road because it is mostly wide sandy beaches and not water. At the last moment we look up and see a long-legged black bird circling over our heads. It makes a harsh sound and turns back to the Great River. We wave goodbye to it. Now Chibwe and I are completely alone.

***

Chibwe and I are facing what we know will be the hardest part of our journey. We walk all day until the early afternoon when we stop to plant the seeds we've brought from the Evergreen Forest. We carefully choose the best place we can for each seed, make a hole for it with Palma's knife and put one drop of water of it from the Source of the Great River. It's slow work but we do it as best as we can. When we finish that task we eat, drink and sleep. Once again, we take it in turn to keep watch during the night in case there are hyenas or other scavengers around.

The further we go, the closer to our home in the Valley, the drier the Sandy River becomes. During the day the bright sun is scorching and the mopane trees are burnt and leafless and give almost no shade. The only birds and animals we see are dead and the land is littered with white bones and dry grey sticks. Soon we find there's no water in the riverbed just sand

and hot round stones. We dig holes in the sand for water, but each day we have to dig deeper and we find less. Every day we're hungrier and thirstier, but we keep on walking day after day up the dry river bed. The only sound we hear is the crackle of dry leaves underfoot.

Makemba told us that when the Drought Witch is destroyed, all the seeds we've planted will grow into trees and replace those that died in the drought. It's harder and harder to believe that will happen.

I'm more and more afraid of the Drought Witch and so is Chibwe.

"How's it possible to get close enough to kill her with a splash of water?" I ask Chibwe.

He shrugs and doesn't answer. Neither of us knows what we can do. Neither of us can think of a workable plan to destroy Kambili.

Our biggest problem is our drinking water. There is less and less in our bottle. The water for planting the seeds is also disappearing but so are the seeds as we plant them. At least that bag is getting lighter. We have to judge the amount of water for planting the seeds very carefully. We don't want to have seeds left over but we must leave enough water from the Source of the Great River to destroy Kambili.

I know that I'm getting very tired. I don't know how much longer I can carry on walking all day in this heat. I look at Chibwe. He must be tired too but he never says so. I catch him looking at me. I think he looks a little annoyed with me. It's getting harder to keep up with him.

CHAPTER TEN
BAD HUNTING

Every day is hot. Every day we walk and we walk. Every day it gets harder to keep on going. Today I collapse at midday. I can't carry on until the day becomes a little cooler. Chibwe finds us a hollow place under a low bush where a patch of grey dusty shade is free of troublesome creatures. We lie down to rest.

My nose begins to twitch. There's something rotten nearby.

"What is that smell?" Chibwe says, pulling a face. "There's something dead nearby. I wonder what killed it and if it's still eating it."

Chibwe and I always talk very quietly to each other when we are in the bush and we use our eyes to see what's going on around us. It's safer that way.

"We must be careful," I say. "I don't want to be attacked by a lion guarding its food."

Chibwe kneels up to have a look around then drops down and shuffles back under the bush.

"There are some vultures in those trees. I don't know why they aren't eating whatever it is."

"Do you think it's a leopard kill up in a tree?" I ask. "Dead things don't last long in the drought. There are too many starving creatures."

Chibwe and I are also hungry but the smell is disgusting.

"I'm going to have a look," Chibwe says. He sneaks from tree to tree to get a better view but comes back almost at once.

"It's a dead warthog tied to a tree branch. Someone is using it as bait probably to attract lion or leopard. Using bait isn't skilled hunting or animal conservation – it's animal murder!" he says, lying down next to me again. "This is a dangerous place to be. We need to get away from here."

"Who would be doing that?" I ask. "Do you think they're close by and watching their bait?"

We both roll over and look behind us. Chibwe tests the wind.

"The smell of the warthog will be stronger to the south-west so that's where they hope the lion will come from. The hunters will probably lie in wait in the opposite direction. They'll have their jeep parked a little way further back. This kind of hunter is lazy and won't walk very far."

"Do you think they are already here?" I ask.

"Shush! Listen!" Chibwe whispers.

We hear the sound of an engine approaching slowly and cautiously from the direction Chibwe thought was the most likely. We flatten ourselves into the ground under our bush. We could be trapped here for a very long time. The jeep stops and the engine is turned off. There's a sharp sound as a metal object knocks against the jeep. It's very quiet again.

"Two men coming," Chibwe whispers. "One is a hunter, the other not."

One man moves almost silently through the bush. The other is flat-footed and clumsy.

"Ow!" We hear the flat-footed one say in what he thinks is a soft voice. "Weather awfully thweaty. Grasses awfully scratchy.

Wonderful hunting – jolly good fun whatever."

Chibwe and I clutch at each other. We think the other hunter is telling him to be quieter but we can't hear his words.

"Yeth Wabenzi old fellow. Will do better – prometh!" Willy Waffell says.

My face sinks into the sand of our hiding hole. We may as well give up now. We'll never escape from Wabenzi wherever we go, whatever we do. I'm too tired to go on any more. I'm holding Chibwe back. He's trapped because of me.

Perhaps, I think, Chibwe can escape by himself. He must go on alone. He must leave me.

Willy Waffell speaks again.

"Yeth Wabenzi, jolly wonderful work with that big Kambili-Witchy-Woman. Got her sorted making the drought – soon have the land empty for the copper mining what-ho business what! Wonderful wiches promethed to uth, I think. Have to do as Witchy-Woman says – don't you Wabenzi!"

"Shut up!" Wabenzi says. "We're hunting now. Quiet Waffell! This is to give you practice shooting. If these wretched children get back here with Makemba's magic we'll probably have to shoot them. That's what Kambili wants us to do!"

"Yeth – indeed – I prometh!" Waffell says.

It's quiet at last.

I whisper into the earth by my nose.

"Creatures of the earth help us please. This is your earth to keep safe."

Chibwe touches my ear. He's telling me to listen and that's when I hear that particular sound.

It's the sound of millions of tiny feet rustling over dry ground. It's the sound of millions of miniature fires racing through grass. It's the sound of millions of army ants all focussed on eating food. It is the sound of an irresistible force that nothing can stop. It's the sound of concentrated hunger. It's the sound of millions of biting jaws racing to attack any moving creature in their way.

I open my eyes wide. If Chibwe and I are in the path of the army ants we will have no choice but to jump up and run and Wabenzi will shoot us both dead at once. I know I can run if I need to but I can't run fast enough to escape Wabenzi's bullets.

That's when we hear a high, piercing scream followed by a loud angry grunt.

The army ants have found Waffell and Wabenzi first. They've come from behind them and started climbing up the men's boots and legs while they're lying in their ambush. Both men are now up and dancing and slapping at themselves. They are covered with ants and Waffell is shrieking and screaming. The vultures flap up slowly from their trees and circle high over the jumping men.

"Into the jeep," shouts Wabenzi. The two men run to their parked vehicle but that means going back down the road that the ants are using. The ants turn back in a swirling mass around the men's feet. It's hard to drive a jeep and, at the same time, brush ants off your body when they've fastened their jaws into your skin. Wabenzi loses control of the jeep. He bashes into a tree by accident and Willy Waffell screams even louder.

"My arm! My arm's broken! Ow! Ow! Ow!"

The sound of the jeep tells us that it's reversing then it keeps stopping and starting but at least it is getting further and further away from us.

Chibwe and I stand up with care. We walk steadily away from the stinking warthog carcass and the ants and the men in their jeep and go back down to the dry river bed and our task of planting seeds.

CHAPTER ELEVEN
THE DROUGHT WITCH

"I can't go on any more," I tell Chibwe. "My legs have stopped working."

Chibwe sits down by my side.

My head is on the ground. All I want to do is sleep. I try and wet my lips with my tongue but my mouth and throat are dry

"We'll rest a while, Chipo," he says. "It can't be very far now."

I see him tilt the two water bottles experimentally but I know there's almost nothing left in either one.

I want to ask what we'll do when we get to our home and find Kambili is there. I want to ask about Ma and Pa but talking is too difficult.

I want to ask where Wabenzi and Waffell are likely to be but I can't do that either. If Waffell did break his arm then Wabenzi must have taken him to hospital. I hope they aren't anywhere near us.

I touch Chibwe's arm.

"You must go on without me," I say and push gently at him. What I've said sounds like "Oo-muth-o-ou-me."

My words are slurred but Chibwe understands, he shakes his head firmly.

"No Chipo! No! I won't leave you!" he says.

I shut my eyes. Chibwe has made a comfortable place for me to rest under a lucky bean tree. He lifts up my head and gives me some water to drink. It's the last of our drinking water. It's wonderful but it isn't enough. Chibwe knows, and I know, that he has to save the water from the Source of the Great River to destroy Kambili.

Chibwe sits by me for a long time while I rest. I am not sleeping properly because I'm too tired and thirsty,

"This is stupid," I think. "We'll both die if we stay like this."

Chibwe is holding my head up again. There's a very determined look on his face. He's giving me another drink. It's the last drops of the water from the Source of the Great River.

I'm not going to swallow it. I won't swallow, I tell myself but it's heavenly on my parched tongue. I shut my eyes.

Chibwe shouts loudly. He makes a choking sound that goes on and on. There's an earthquake happening. The ground is rocking around me as if an army is stamping up and down and there's shouting and a terrible din.

"The girl's dead! Leave her! I'll kill you! I'll squeeze the breath out of your puny body – you wretched nuisance of a boy." I feel Chibwe being torn from my side. I feel his legs and arms flailing around and accidentally kicking me. I force my eyes open. Kambili is leaning over Chibwe and me. She is huge. She's grown to the size of a buffalo. She has her hands around Chibwe's neck and she's strangling him in her giant hands. His eyes are staring and he is making a terrible sound. I grab at Kambili. I pull myself towards her. I tug at her hands and my face is close to hers.

I spit at her.

I spit the last precious drops of the water from the Source

of the Great River from out of my mouth into her face.

"Let my brother go!" I scream.

Kambili's eyes get bigger and bigger and closer and closer to me. I feel I going to be sucked up into their spinning yellow voids.

She explodes. Yes, she explodes.

She's nothing but the dust of the whirlwind she arrived in and now she's only dust and grime spinning and blowing away.

I'm knocked over and winded but Chibwe is standing up. He's alive. He's gasping for air, but he's alive.

"Chibwe!" I shout.

"Chipo!" he says, hoarsely.

CHAPTER TWELVE
THIS IS WHAT HAPPENED AFTER WE GOT HOME

The end of the Drought Witch, Kambili, is only the beginning of the story of Chibwe and me. It's the start of our lives and of all the things we still have to do and learn. First of all, we have to go back to school. We are a whole year behind the other students and we need to catch up fast.

That's rushing on a bit, though.

When Chibwe and I stood up in the dust left by Kambili's destruction we felt that some of our strength had come back to us. I suppose we were rather shocked that her end had come so unexpectedly, just when we had almost given up. We were still hungry, thirsty and rather weak but we weren't afraid of her any more and we wanted to get home to find our parents. We couldn't be sure that Kambili hadn't killed them because she had destroyed so many animals and trees and plants in the Valley. We didn't dare hope too much as our journey had been so long and so difficult.

We discovered once we set off again, that we weren't very far from the farm anyway, but when we got there, we found the farmhouse and the yard were empty. There was nothing growing in the fields and no one to be seen.

"Ma, Pa!" we called.

I thought I heard the faint sound of a voice.

"Where's the grain store?" Chibwe said, looking round.

227

"Look over there!" I said. "The termites have built a huge earth castle around the grain store! They must have made that in a very short time!"

"That's where the voices are coming from," Chibwe said. "It's a magic prison made by Kambili. Ma and Pa are inside it."

Chibwe and I tried to break the termite mound down but we couldn't manage it at all. We were almost in despair. What we hadn't noticed in all the excitement of Kambili's hideous appearance and explosive departure was the change in the weather. Huge thunderheads had appeared in the sky and a moist wind had started to blow towards us from the Evergreen Forest so far away in the North-West. We were still scratching at the surface of the termite mound and calling out to Pa and Ma when a heavy rain started to fall. Rain is the best and most wonderful gift of all. We stood there with our eyes shut and our tongues out, drinking the rain and getting soaked. We thanked the Rain Spirits and Makemba and we thought of Mokoro and Imbolondo and the kindness of so many people we'd met on our journey. While we were drinking up the falling rain the termite mound was dissolving away. When we turned back to the grain store, we found Ma and Pa waking up from the spell that Kambili had cast on them.

We hugged and we cried and we talked and we did that again and again over the next few weeks. We all had to recover our health and our strength and we had to look after each other. We also had so much to do to get the fields and the garden ready for planting. We had to heal the damaged earth and look after the trees and see that the river was running free again and that the trees were not cut down on the river banks.

We had to pay our respects to the Spirits of our Ancestors. We had to visit Grandmother and phone Aunt Chimunya and Faith. We had to invite Masika to come and visit us. He did visit us, and finally he decided that he would come and live with Grandmother.

We would have to start an important campaign to stop Mr Wabenzi and Mr Waffell's plan to start mining for copper in our Valley.

That first night of, course, there was no food left in the house. We didn't starve, however. The rain had brought us yet another gift. That night, as usually happens after rain, the new termite queens found their wings and left their nests. One by one, they flew into our frying pan until it was full. On our first night together, after all our adventures, Ma, Pa, Chibwe and I had a delicious and nutritious meal of fried termites.

ACKNOWLEDGEMENTS

John Corley for his unstinting patience, editing and support. Sandra Glover of Cornerstones for helping me turn the book into a story for middle-graders. Nikki Ashley for the best possible editing. Tia and Eyal Azulay for my website and for believing in my stories. Angel Phiri for all kinds of advice about Zambia. Joel Bossiaux for help with digital images. St Martin's School of Art for teaching me how to begin my story. Everyone in my family for their interest and kindness. Zambians and those who love to make gardens and Zambia for its rich natural resources. Friends who read my story and commented on it. And finally to Fay Gadsden of Gadsden Publishers for taking the risk that publishing a story always involves.

This book was begun twenty seven years ago as an urgent project to raise environmental awareness. During that period, I've consulted too many friends to list you all. I'm in your debt. This story is I believe, more important than ever.